# *The* BOY *in the* BURGUNDY HOOD

*A Ghost Story*

STEVE GRIFFIN

*by Steve Griffin*

FICTION

*The Secret of the Tirthas series:*

The City of Light
The Book of Life
The Dreamer Falls
The Lady in the Moon Moth Mask
The Unknown Realms

POETRY

Up in the Air

She is running, as fast as she can, across the great lawn towards the lake.

She can see the long branch, snapped halfway out across the water. Behind her, she hears shouts. Panic makes her lurch, nearly lose her footing on the grass.

She knows what has happened, ever since she heard the great cracking sound, the splash, through the open bedroom window.

What are they doing here? She should never have left him to play alone in this place.

As she comes up the bank she halts, stunned that her worst imagining - that it's true. Simply true.

Amidst the shapeless tangle of the broken branch he floats, face down in the water. He is wearing that anorak, the one she's told him not to wear in the summer heat, but which he wears regardless. It's like a shield. A shield skin for him.

She screams his name, once, twice, again.

Behind her, the man arrives, plunges into the water, swims out to bring the boy back in.

He shouts too, but there's no response. The boy moves gently with the eddies caused by the man's swimming, just like the broken branch. She notices one of his pumps, one of his dirty old pumps, is missing. Showing his sock, incongruous, odd, like a lump of grey chalk in the water.

Moments later, the man drags the boy out on to the bank.

'I shouldn't have done it,' she says, as the man covers the boy's mouth with his own, trying to resuscitate him. 'I should never have left him alone in this place...' She looks up at the sky, around at the woods, the lawn, glances back at the old, timbered house. She can't look down, can't bear to see the soggy whiteness of his little face.

After a while, she hears a dog barking, becomes aware of more movement behind her.

The man kneels up from the boy and his expression confirms the worst. The absolute worst. It can't be... no, it can't be...

Then the man looks past her to the other who is approaching.

'I think we need to do it now, pater,' he says.

## The Ideal Candidate

1

'Ideal. You were the ideal candidate. Totally.'

Alice smiled, her head tipped down a little towards the coffee Fran had made her. *I'd rather be gardening*, said the cup, with a silhouette of a watering can by a shed.

'Really, you were,' said Fran, beaming back at her from across the kitchen table.

'Thanks. I didn't know what on earth they made of me.' Alice thought back to her interview in the early summer.

'The dear old Smythe-Johnstones? They loved you.'

'Really? How could you tell?' Alice sipped the coffee and realised that Fran had forgotten the sugar. 'They asked some unusual questions.'

'Of course. They are nosy old parkers. They just wanted to make sure you weren't going to throw wild parties as soon as you moved in.'

'Like the last one?'

'No. She was quiet as a mouse. The place just didn't suit her.'

'I wondered about the smoking question you asked in the first part of the interview, the bit without them. Was that based on a real scenario?'

'*You come back one night and find the owners have a friend round who's smoking in the dining room?* Previous owners, I should say.'

'Yes. Did it happen? I thought it might have led to an argument with my predecessor.'

'No, I made that up. The one about the high heels on the parquet flooring was true, though.'

Alice laughed. She'd admired Fran from the moment she met her. Forthright, solid, decisive, wry, insightful. She was everything she imagined a Regional Manager – or *RM* – of the Trust for England to be. Qualities she planned to inhabit herself now, in her new role.

'I'm so pleased you chose me,' she said.

'You're very welcome. I think you're going to love it here. I really do. Just remember who's boss.'

2

She closed the door to Bramley on Fran, hearing the RM's footsteps crunch away across the gravel of the short moat bridge.

She locked the door – or gate, more accurately – using its old black iron key. There was resistance in there, the bit twisting against the lock, the bow hard against her knuckle. For a moment she thought it would hurt. And then it moved with sudden ease and the house was shut.

With her, Alice Deaton, on the inside.

She smiled. What would Matthew think?

A new job, new beginning...

She continued to hold the key, her other hand pressed against the ridged, weathered wood of the door panel.

She got the job. She was here. In a medieval manor house, owned by the Trust for England. And *she* was the boss.

Oh my God.

Oh my good God.

She was smiling. Smiling to herself.

She turned and walked a few paces beneath the stone passageway and past the two laurel bushes that framed the open courtyard. On the left was the Tudor wing with its timber frames and dun plastering, with a gold clock beneath the highest pitched roof. Straight ahead was the larger and earlier stone block of the Great Hall with its narrow, chapel-like windows. In the centre of the cobbled yard was a group of stone planters, full of untidy box shrubs.

It was magnificent. Completely magnificent. And entrusted to her.

And still, she supposed, to the *dear old Smythe-Johnstones.*

She stood, feeling a mix of apprehension and excitement. Were they here now? She assumed they were, there was a clapped-out Aston Martin parked up by one of the outhouses (one that she had already clocked as the most appropriate for conversion into the ticket office, adjacent to an open area by the high wall which would make a good car park). She scanned the windows, dull grey in the autumn light. There. The lights in their apartment, in the corner on the right, the south-west corner, were a wan, muted gold like dessert wine. Alice loved the invitation and warmth of that light, puncturing the bleak medieval wall. She felt again the age of this place, its ancient inheritance, which had so impressed her when she came for the interview in July, a different season when the flowers were blooming and the birds warbling in the trees. Any moment, you expected a man in a red velvet doublet and hose to appear, or a maid in coif and apron.

She gazed at the apartment windows for a moment but there was no sign of the house's owners. *Previous* owners. How awful for them, she thought, as she crossed the cobbles to the Great Hall entrance. After two hundred years in the family, to have to swallow your pride and hand it over to an institution.

Still, at least there *was* a Trust for England. Better than selling it off to a private developer and finding your ancestral home converted into a hotel and conference centre.

And at least that meant they were able to stay.

3

The first thing that struck her as she closed the outside door to the vestibule was the silence.

The only natural light came from the open doorway into the Great Hall, feeble at this time of year, so she flicked on the electric lights. A small chandelier pressed milky, yellowish light into the shadows. The entrance hall was small, oak-panelled, with that peculiar sense of solidity that only low stone ceilings and history can create. There were interesting items in the vestibule, a lovely wrought-iron umbrella stand and some gold-framed miniature folk art of farm animals, sows, horses, sheep – but the irresistible draw was the Great Hall, where Alice could glimpse the giant hearth and a fine suit of plate armour. She hurried through.

Even in the mid-afternoon gloom, Bramley's grandest room was stunning. Alice turned slowly around, gazing up at the vaulted ceiling, the great mullioned windows, a dark, giant tapestry at the far end. In the centre of the hall was a huge table, unlaid, with elegant chairs along its length.

She moved towards the fireplace, a good fifteen-foot-long, observing the giant portrait of a Victorian gentleman above it. He was a portly-looking fellow, partially bald, chestnut hair in retreat around his ears. His eyes were pale blue, gazing across at the vast window with a strange, visionary passion.

Wondering who he might have been, Alice moved down the room, noticing the glass lanterns hung on twenty-foot chains, the worn red-and-gold heraldic rug, a long seat like an Elizabethan pew against one wall. For a moment she felt acutely her lack of expertise, realising she had little idea of the heritage value of much in the room. She wondered if such things would come back to haunt her, if Fran would soon realise she'd appointed someone with huge gaps in her knowledge.

She moved on quickly, exiting the Hall through the far door to escape a growing queasiness in her stomach.

You can do this, she told herself.


4


Her butterflies subsided as she came up the western staircase to the first floor. She passed the Smythe-Johnstone's apartments – effectively most of the west wing of the building, their door marked private – and headed down the landing.

About halfway down that long, narrow corridor she saw the boy.

He was up ahead in the gloom, a flash of burgundy between the latticed windows and the dark satin of the panelled walls. He was gone, away, up a step and off down the next corridor as quick as she saw him.

Was he real? Had she imagined him?

She walked quickly along the landing, her trainers squeaking on the floorboards.

'Hello?' she called.

At the step she looked down the next passage. There was a gallery bannister overlooking a second stairwell, and further on doors to two bedrooms – one of which was hers. There was no one there. The corridor turned at the end, towards the chapel and priest's room.

Did the Smythe-Johnstones have a child? Or, more likely, a grandchild? He was wearing a modern anorak with a hood, that was the flash of red she had seen. She was sure Fran said they had very few remaining relatives. There was a long-lost son and a daughter apparently, but she lived up North and rarely visited.

Alice made a quick sweep of the wing, the small, musty chapel with its stained-glass window of a blue-robed Jesus with lamb, and the simple grey vault of the priest's room, with its attached garderobe, relatively bare except for a single, sagging bed and a couple of chairs that looked like they had come out of a classroom. Above the bed was a solitary painting of a woman in a field.

There was no one there, few places to hide, and no other way out. Had the boy gone down the galleried stairs? He could just about have made it, although not quietly.

Bramley's first mystery. Alice smiled. Briefly, she wondered whether she should continue her search downstairs. Supposing some intrepid local schoolboy had managed to sneak into the building, perhaps whilst Fran had left the gate open as they made their tour? Maybe she should go straight to the Smythe-Johnstone's apartments – S-Js, Smythe-Johnstone is such a thought-full, she would call them the S-Js – and check with them. They could confirm whether he was with them. Or whether he was a renowned local pest. Or the house's resident ghost.

Or just something Alice's ridiculously-racing, overactive imagination had devised on her first solitary journey between the venerable, history-soaked walls of Bramley. It wouldn't be the first time she'd imagined something that wasn't there.

She would leave it. She didn't want to create a bad first impression. Asking about imaginary kids on her first day could quickly undermine her authority with the dear old S-Js.

5

The next morning, Alice woke to the sound of a dog barking.

There was already a creeping light in her bedroom as she'd forgotten to draw the heavy curtains. She lay there, wiggling her toes against the sheets and marvelling at the carved posts of her bed, the grey silk sheet of the canopy above her. The mattress was old, springy, sloping towards the middle – but still she had slept soundly. She had expected not to sleep a wink with the excitement, but it was so peaceful here. The silence was so profound, so alien to her normal experience, it almost felt like a presence. A presence entwined with the building itself, with its reassuring power – the power of its history and the privileged people who had lived within its walls. Having slept little the week before in her one bed flat in Farnborough, she was amazed now to feel so refreshed. What an unexpected gift.

She looked around at her quarters, at the old bureau in the corner and the blue IKEA-looking couch – the one modern piece of furniture in the whole building – facing the fireplace. A fireplace she would never be able to light, unfortunately, because of Trust rules. You didn't want a seven-hundred-year-old house razed to the ground because some poor little property manager was feeling the cold. On the wall opposite there was a huge grey tapestry, an appropriately drab Tudor hunting scene.

From outside, there came another throaty woof.

Was that the Smythe-Johnstone's – the S-J's – dog? she wondered. Then she heard dimly, away across the quadrangle, a woman's voice. Elderly, cultured, calling out a few words that started in a tone of command but seemed to trail off ineffectually as the dog barked again. Undoubtedly Mrs S-J. Samantha.

Alice got up and dressed in her khaki trousers and yellow fleece. No uniform yet, although she had mentioned to Fran how she thought it would be good to get one soon as part of the drip feed to the S-Js that things were on the verge of major change. Seeing her in the Trust for England green, badged with the ubiquitous antlered stag, would be another sign that authority over Bramley's future had shifted. Forever.

She unlatched her door and went downstairs to the kitchen where she made herself tea and toast. She had to eat the toast dry as she'd forgotten to buy any butter.

The weather was good – a mild day, windy, with muted sunshine – so she decided to head straight out, to get a feel for the building exterior and the grounds. Fran had explained that there was still no full business plan for the house. There was a development plan, of which some of the works had already been done. These included emergency repairs to the withdrawing room roof, as well as basic adaptations for moving the S-Js to their own apartment and for setting up Alice's living quarters (at the moment, one of the bedrooms, a small downstairs cloakroom now to be her office, and the kitchen). Whilst they were still working on the business plan back at headquarters, Fran had made her own list of urgent, very urgent and absolutely-bloody-urgent-so-do-it-now tasks. Such, according to the RM, was the state of the building and its importance to the nation, that there were no tasks that could be marked low importance.

Fran wanted Alice to spend her first few days just looking around, soaking the place up. She wanted her to make her own judgements on what she thought were the most important things to do before the 'first stage', low-key, opening next spring. Alice knew it was a test. The Trust must have realised they were taking a gamble, appointing someone with a Masters in Conservation Studies (specialist subject, Textiles), a six-month stint as a volunteer in Watt's Gallery, and two years as an assistant manager in a community centre. To be honest, she was still amazed that she had got the job. She wondered what the other candidates were like, that skinny guy before her, the one with the spots who looked as if he was just out of school. Surely some experienced Property Manager would kill for a live-in post like this?

Maybe it was all to do with the S-Js themselves. Perhaps word in the network was that they had driven the first incumbent insane, steer clear of that one, not worth the day-to-day conflict and misery. And it was just her, naïve little Alice Deaton, who had walked into it undefended.

Then again, no. What was the point of thinking like that?

Things had not been good lately – not been good for a long time, in fact, ever since her mother died – and this was the chance for a brand new start.

And she, Alice Deaton, had got the job precisely because she was the best person for the job. The one who, as the application had asked in its roundabout way, would not be put off by long periods away from friends and family in a remote location. But also the one with just the right skill set, maybe just below the hoped-for level of experience, but certainly with the right level of passion for place. And ambition, of course. She was dead set on making this one work. *Dead* set.

The ideal candidate, just as Fran had said.

6

She spent the morning walking the grounds, exploring the walled kitchen garden, the great lawn to the east with its green lake that fed the house's small moat, the denuded woods that clacked in the wind around the lake. She imagined the army of volunteers she would need to recruit to get it all back into shape; the mowing, weeding, pollarding, edging and gravelling that had to be done. And done again. And again. And again.

One step at a time.

A few years back she'd visited Lemington House in the Surrey Hills, the former home of an esoteric clergyman and renowned amateur naturalist, which was one of the more recent Trust houses to open. She remembered exploring the dark lanes of laurel and rhododendron with her mum, how she'd helped her when she'd wandered from the path and shoved a foot in a muddy ditch. She cleaned her mum's pink trainer as best she could with leaves and a single, crumpled tissue and then, after a moment of weighing it up, decided not to abort the trip early.

She was glad she hadn't. The volunteer on the door, a lady whose glamorous bob was the only thing brightening the day, could have talked forever about the challenges of making the house ready for the public. She explained the Trust's initial uncertainty about opening the doors after their previous tenants had left, because of the enormous costs involved; the difference made by an innovative call for volunteers in the local towns and villages; the brainstorming sessions on the house's history to find which stories would most appeal to visitors; the testing of the place's appeal through a trial opening; and much more. Alice had been aware that all the time the lady was speaking her mum had been staring at a painting, a woman in a green chiffon dress with tight orange curls atop her white forehead. Her mum didn't seem to be taking much in from the portrait, but at least she was stable, lost in its mysterious interaction with her thoughts.

Yes, Alice was glad she'd taken her mum into the house because that ebullient steward had given her three of her best answers to the questions she'd had in her interview.

And because it was the last trip she'd ever had with her mum.

7

She had been wondering who was doing the gardening now. As she came back through a small orchard on an incline above the house she found out.

To the right of the muddy path was a dark, shallow bank of yew trees. In the midst of these was a strange, dank area that had the feel of a rockery or grotto – and in the midst of that, digging, was a solitary figure.

His broad shoulders were hunched away from her, so she couldn't see his face. He was attacking the ground with some gusto, lifting the spade above his head before each strike, emitting a small grunt that was echoed by the tinny scrape of the blade in the soil. His hair was dark, curly as if permed; he was in old, ripped chinos and a shabby sweater with a reddish leather patch on one sleeve.

'Hello.'

He stopped for a moment and coughed twice. Then carried on digging.

'Hello,' she said again. The man continued to dig.

Was he ignoring her?

'Hi, I'm Alice, the new property manager,' she said again, walking towards him. As she drew nearer she realised the unusual feature wasn't a rockery or grotto, but a collection of uprooted, mossy tree stumps, arranged at varying angles. They were like alien creatures, something that would be at home in a dalek suit. There was a word for this feature.

As she drew nearer to the man he suddenly stopped and twisted around. There was a look of apprehension, a cornered look in the eyes that met hers from beneath the shaggy black fringe.

'Alice...' she said and offered her hand.

The anxiety faded from the man's face and was quickly replaced by a smile. Or a half smile. A shy smile. He pushed the spade into the ground and shook her hand.

Then he pointed at his mouth and ears and shook his head.

Alice nodded.

'It's a stumpery, isn't it?' she said, remembering.

The young man smiled and raised his thumb.

'I'm the new property manager,' she said.

He nodded and mouthed something, squeezing out a strained whimper. Alice tilted her head, trying not to exaggerate her action. It has been a long time since she'd met someone who was deaf and dumb. He might as well have told her his name was Cornelius for all she'd understood. She tried a face that was helpless, but not too helpless. She didn't want to patronise or offend him.

He lifted a finger to hold her attention. Then he picked up the spade handle in one hand, stood up straight, lifted his chin and ceremoniously slid the spade down past his hip and along his leg. He lifted a leg and pretended to mount a horse, made a surprisingly good pretence of galloping along. Then he switched around one-hundred-and-eighty degrees, lifted his arms and flapped them like wings, undulating his back. Whilst still flapping his left arm, he pushed a mass of wriggling fingers away from his mouth with the other hand.

'Hello, George,' she said.

George smiled. A full smile this time, showing his teeth.

'Have you been here long?'

He raised his fingers, less his left-hand pinky.

'Nine years,' said Alice. 'That's great.'

He nodded.

'I look forward to... to working with you.'

She would have liked to say more, but a momentary anxiety seized her and she didn't want to show it. What else could she say that wouldn't require a simple yes-no answer? Would he want to stay on with a new boss in the manor?

Feeling a heat on her face she said: 'It's nice to meet you, perhaps we can...'

He pinched the forefinger and thumb of his right hand together, seemed to kiss them, and then mimed writing on his left palm.

'Yes, we'll get a pen and paper next time,' she said. He touched his forehead in an understated salute and turned back to his digging in the tentacle-swarm of the stumpery.

8

'I met George this morning.'

Samantha Smythe-Johnstone looked at her blankly.

'The gardener?'

'Oh – George, is it,' said the woman, flicking her eyes up at the grey-panelled ceiling of the library. The library that was as much a series of rooms within a room, with its subdivided sections along the far wall where people could read, study or take an afternoon nap in front of a steel stove. It was quickly becoming one of Alice's favourite rooms.

'Yes… the mute.'

'Mute?'

'Yes.'

Samantha smiled at her, but it was pinched, almost fawned.

'He said he's been here nine years, he must be a real asset.'

'An asset, yes. Indubitably.'

Samantha took a sip of tea whilst Alice, opposite her across a small table by the stove, tried to keep Henry's flews away from her trousers. It was hopeless, the Lab had already made them look like they'd been out overnight in a slug-infested garden.

'His father used to help out before him,' Samantha volunteered, after she had reset her cup in the Wedgewood saucer. Alice noticed chips on the rim, well past her mum's limit for chucking. 'The family is local. Loveton.'

Alice nodded. 'I passed through it on the way,' she said.

'He lives alone now. A friend used to live with him. He also worked as a gardener, up at Forthill, but he had carcinoma. One of the bad ones, all over his back before he realised. He never looked in a mirror and didn't have a wife or girlfriend. Both were real outdoor types, they couldn't stand being cooped up inside at all. It wouldn't happen these days of course, not with all that cream everyone slops on… Henry, come away!'

Henry's tongue or flew or nose or all three slavered across the back of Alice's hand as she tried to shove him away.

'He's OK,' she said, chuckling feebly.

'Come away, you bad boy!'

Henry turned his droopy eyes towards his mistress. Most Labs showed considerable intelligence, Alice thought, but not this one. He didn't appear bad natured, he was just struggling to keep up. Under the power of Samantha S-J's stare he finally cottoned on to what was required of him and sidled off to collapse beneath one of the windows of the long room.

Alice had met Samantha on her return to the house after her encounter with George. Mrs S-J had just got back from walking Henry and suggested a cup of tea. Bernard S-J had driven into town to buy some essentials, she had informed Alice.

'I'd just like to say, thank you so much for putting your trust in me,' said Alice, after they had both turned back to one another.

'That's quite all right. We're looking forward to working with you.'

Alice smiled. *Working with* was good, at least at this stage.

'I've been thinking about the rich history of the place,' she said. 'The different phases of construction, the negotiations that took place here in the Civil War, the antics of Goodyear, the derelict period at the beginning of the eighteenth century. There's so much. What are your favourite episodes from Bramley's past?'

Samantha looked at her. Whilst her sclera were yellowing there was no sign of decline in the button-brown eyes that scrutinised the young woman before her. The sixties were still young after all these days. For some people, Alice thought, remembering her mum.

'My great-grandfather, Forbes, was a keen classicist,' said the woman. 'There's a portrait of him in the Great Hall, above the fireplace. He spent years in Italy, in Ostia Antica and other places, working with archaeologists. He was a character, built a ladder so he could swim in the moat every day, even when he had to break through ice. He thought so much had been lost since the start of western culture. Brought back some of the house's best pieces.'

She looked up at the mantelpiece. Alice first thought she was looking at the clock, then realised she was gazing at a large painting of a bull above it.

'Is that something he brought back?'

'Yes. I've no idea of the artist but Bernard believes it's seventeenth century. Look at the eyes.'

Alice stood up to examine the painting more closely. She thought she was being side-lined in her questioning. But at least the painting provided a way out of the awkwardness.

She examined the bull. His muscular, off-white body reminded her of a landscape painting, like a mountain in the middle of the picture. The power of a mountain, of nature. She could feel it, for a moment it was like a small shock, the shock of awe, behind the eyes. His expression, tilting one eye toward the artist, was calculating, sour, ready to destroy, not with a mad rush but with the comprehensive certainty of an avalanche. No escape.

'His crown's magnificent,' she said, studying the wavy cream locks piled around its small horns.

'You do textiles, don't you?' said Samantha.

23

'Yes.' Alice turned away from the painting. 'I did an MA in textile conservation.'

'I remember from the interview. We have something we hope you could take a look at some time.'

'No problems, I'd love to. What is it?'

'Another Italian piece brought back by my great-grandfather. A tapestry that's got a bad stain. Would you see what you think?'

'Of course.'

Samantha's eyes shone with goodwill.

'I think you will be much better than the last one,' she said. Her small eyes flicked towards the window. 'Silly little mouse…'

Alice, who had been on the verge of saying she was pleased, pulled back a little in surprise. 'Oh…' she said.

Samantha looked back from the window. For a moment she looked confused, then her expression became warm again. Fake warm.

'Sorry. We didn't get on with her very well. I'm sure you heard.'

'A little,' said Alice. 'What were the issues?' She hadn't been planning to go here, but best to *strike while the iron* etc.

'What do they call it these days? Passive-aggressive. There would be nothing out of her for weeks on end, then one day she'd appear and demand we kept ourselves to our quarters, not come down and use what is, after all, our own house.'

Alice stayed silent, a trick she'd learnt from her mum. Let them talk when they were talking.

'Bramley has been in our family for over two hundred and fifty years, after all. We have made it what it is. We have found ways to keep it going, to make it survive.'

Alice nodded her head slowly. Keep going.

But cognition showed in the woman's expression, as if she understood the game Alice was playing. 'Don't get me wrong,' she said, her shoulders relaxing. 'We aren't old fools, we understand the new reality. We couldn't afford the best lawyer to go through the minutiae, but we fully intend to abide by the agreement. After nearly three centuries, the place is no longer truly ours. We can't pretend to be happy about it, but we don't intend to make your life difficult, or blame you for it in anyway.'

Alice tried to keep calm. This was way more than she'd been expecting from a chat over tea. Half a dozen potential responses to this strange but probably highly honest little outpour raced through her mind but she ended up on the simplest.

'Thank you,' she said.

9

In the afternoon it became clear to her just how much Bramley was on its knees.

She made a slow tour of all the rooms, starting on the ground floor. She began with a careful scan of the state of the rooms, checking the panelling, floorboards and plaster. There were fearsome cracks in the ceilings in the kitchen, the Housekeeper's room and the Butler's pantry. The one in the pantry she could put her fist through, it was that wide. Besides the wear and tear of ordinary use over aeons, the floorboards and some of the wall panelling were riddled with woodworm. She would need to seek the conservators' advice on what could be saved and what would have to go. One thing she was pleased of, there might be a musty smell but there was little sign of proper damp – an irony, considering the house was surrounded by water. Someone was evidently paying good attention to cleaning and repairing the lead gutters.

The S-Js didn't have the funds or personal energy to keep the building clean and tidy. A few rooms were clearly favourites – the library, Great Hall and, to a lesser extent, the small dining room – but all the others were dirty, dusty, filled with bric-a-brac that could just as easily have contained priceless chattels as junk. Whilst the place was fascinating, Alice's slow, steady progress through the rooms began to make her feel increasingly depressed. With few exceptions (mainly in the library), upholstery and textiles were in a particularly poor state, most having lost a considerable amount of fibre and pigment. The hunting tapestry in her room, which only this morning she had thought in need of emergency repair, turned out to be in better condition than all the other tapestries. There was a small hanging of fruit and veg near the fire in the Great Hall, probably early fifteenth century, which would have been worth thousands, but had been damaged irrevocably by soot from its poor positioning. She doubted it would fetch a few hundred quid now. The library held a reasonable collection of books, many in a good state. *Macaulay's History of England, The Science of Facial Expression,* a load of Westerns and early editions of most of Ian Fleming's James Bond novels – the first of which, *Moonraker,* she opened and found signed by the author:

*To Charles,*
*Bramley is the best, thanks for a wild weekend –*
*Ian*

She had no idea how much, but they would definitely be worth something to a collector.

The paintings were divided into two camps. There were those that had suffered a lot of light damage due to their proximity to large windows, especially those in the Great Hall and library, which faced south. Many of the paintings in the dimmest rooms had suffered buckling and draws; quite a few frames had also been ravaged by woodworm (she imagined Bramley as a party house for the little critters – come on over, guys, this is the place to be!)

Then there were those paintings that seemed to be looked after more carefully, their varnish might be yellowing but they had been kept away from too much light and even dusted. It occurred to her as she inspected that the most care had been taken with those pictures she imagined Forbes might have brought back from Italy, the set pieces of Jupiter, Neptune and other Roman gods, as well as more pastoral scenes and portraits. And, of course, the portrait of the great man himself, hanging above the fireplace, which was in pristine condition.

She came through a second, smaller courtyard past the crypt into a small hall with stairs up to the second floor and doors to the scullery and kitchen. She ascended the stairs and turned sharp right down the landing away from the door that gave access to the S-J's wing. She couldn't help slowing a little, to see if she could hear them. But there was nothing, not a sound, so she carried on alongside the leaded windows that looked down across the quadrangle. She slowed a little, realising that this was where she had seen the boy in the hood the day before.

But today there was no one, no flash of colour or imagined presence.

The chapel was one of the few uncluttered rooms. A congealed layer of dust covered the pews and the prayer books had sagged sadly into the trays in which they were propped. The altar was covered in a stained white cloth, and didn't even display a cross. The S-Js were clearly not spending their Sunday mornings here anymore.

Finally she came back into the priest's room, bare except for a couple of boxes, the bed, and wooden chairs. She walked over to the solitary painting of the old woman. The room was gloomy, it was nearly six and the sun was probably down, so she shook her phone to light up its torch and take a better look at it.

It took her a moment to make sense of the painting. At first she thought the old dairy woman in black was leading a cow away into the landscape. But a closer look showed that the cow's head was risen towards the woman. Whilst she was almost completely turned away from the viewer, Alice could see a pink smudge that – upon even closer look – she realised was one of her breasts, which she appeared to be proffering to the beast.

An old woman, suckling a cow? Hardly the kind of thing you'd expected in a priest's room, she thought.


10


'So what they like?'

'I haven't seen him again yet. But I had tea with her this morning.'

'Lady Smythe-Johnstone.'

'Not a Lady, no, just an ordinary commoner like you and me.'

'Wish I had her money.'

'They haven't got any money. That's why we've taken it over.'

Talking to Matthew on the phone, Alice felt a little kick of excitement, describing the Trust for England as *we* for the first time.

Matthew's voice warped and crackled. '…'

'I can't hear you. The reception's terrible. Can you hear me?'

In the end she hung up. She went into the tiny room with a sink off her bedroom, the garderobe, and leaned into the little window that faced east over the lawn. It was black outside now, of course, but in the dim light of the ancient-looking overhead bulb she saw the reception bars jiggle between one and three, before finally settling on two. She tried again.

'You were saying?' she said.

'What was she like?'

'Old. A little prickly. But I think ultimately a realist. With a revolting dog.'

'Why?'

'Slobbers everywhere.'

'What?'

'I said – he slobbers everywhere.'

'Lobsters? What's lobsters got to do with it?'

'I said he *slobbers everywhere!*'

Matthew chuckled. 'I got you,' he said.

'How's the Centre?'

'…broke down the other night. Mike is still a butt. I don't think… break even again this year.'

'Not again?'

'No. The Adult Ed contract is down for the last term. The council facing more emergency cuts. They've dropped some of the English language courses.'

'Shit. What does Mandy say? Any redundancies looming?'

'No permanent contracts. Likely some of the teaching staff.'

'Not such a disaster then.'

'What? You've gone on me ag…'

Alice watched her phone, the bars had vanished but the call was still connected, still connected, still… gone.

She needed to talk to Fran about the landline. At the moment they'd agreed she would use her mobile – the Trust would reimburse the bill – but it was no good if reception was rubbish. They wouldn't be able to share the S-J's line (assuming they had one), so they would have to get their own put in. A reliable phone – and email, for that matter – were going to be essential very soon to liaise with all those staff, volunteers and contractors. How had her predecessor managed?

She decided there was no point calling Matthew again and went back into her room. She looked around at her meagre furnishings. The room had been very chilly when she first came back up, but it had heated up now thanks to the electric oil heater Fran had dug out for her. (The old iron radiators of Bramley's antiquated central heating system were shut down throughout most of the house, and struggled to make an impact in the few rooms in which they were on). Still, she kept her fleece on with a jumper over top. She felt like a Womble. She wondered how it was going to be in the depths of the winter, before the Trust could service the system and bring it up to the standard needed for thousands of elderly visitors. With all the other urgent, very urgent and absolutely-bloody-urgent-so-do-it-now tasks, she'd be surprised to see it fixed this year. Knuckle down and get used to some cold, Deaton.

She switched on the reading light – a pretty little Victorian lampshade with ochre tassels – and sat down on the couch in front of the fireplace. She breathed out, long and hard, realising how exhausted she was. She'd been on her feet all day, her mind racing – exploding would be a better word – with ideas. Now it was – she checked her phone – 8.52, and she was pooped. Absolutely buggered. She picked up her book, a historical mystery set amongst the first power stations on Niagara Falls – and her phone rang again.

It was Matthew.

'The reception's rubbish here,' she said. 'It might be easier if we communicate by text.'

'Yes,' he said. 'I was just going to say, shall I come up and see you?'

There was a fraction of a pause before she said: 'Yes.'

Another millisecond of silence. 'Great. When?'

'Well, when would you like?'

There was another distortion, something that fuzzed and sounded like a robot saying *wow, wow, wowz*.

'Sorry?' she said.

'…two weekend's time? On the Saturday. The… eenth?'

'What – the fifteenth? Yes, sure – look, that would be great. Send me a text and I can confirm it with the boss.'

She hung up and stared at the china bull on the mantelpiece. The S-Js in their original grilling of her had been very keen to know about her private life. Early on in the discussion they had established – with appropriate sympathetic nods and platitudes – that her parents had both passed away, and that she lived on her own in a rented flat in Farnborough. They commiserated with her story of selling the family house to pay for her mum's care. A little later, Samantha had had to apologise on behalf of her husband when he asked whether Alice had a boyfriend. She'd told them no, quite correctly.

But now things had changed. Kind of.

When she'd handed her notice in at Albany Park community centre and started informing the staff, Matthew, the part-time bookkeeper, had asked her to go mountain biking with him. She'd agreed and they'd had a great time bombing through the fresh, piney glades of the common. Afterwards they had gone for a drink and a curry back in town and then… well then, she had all of a sudden found herself in a relationship, something very exciting, certainly the sex, it had been a year since her last fling and three years since her last – and short-lived – and *only* – boyfriend. But she was also aware how that excitement was also threatening to be lost under the tsunami of thoughts and feelings about her new job.

She wondered – briefly – how Bernard S-J, with his long jaw and oddly flexible eyebrows, like a pair of hairy caterpillars on drugs, would have reacted if she'd told him she had a boyfriend. He was a bit *too* over-familiar in interview. She hoped he wasn't pervy, getting vicarious pleasure from discussing a young woman's love life. Would he have been happier or sadder if she were in a relationship?

And now, having spoken to Matthew, she suddenly wondered: how did *she* feel about being in a relationship?

She didn't sleep half as well on her second night.

For a long time, she struggled to get warm in bed. She eventually clambered out from between the twisted covers and fumbled on woolly socks and a long-sleeved T-shirt over her pyjama top. Shortly after that she did fall asleep (sometime after 12) but she was woken several times on the cusp of strange, vivid dreams that she was certain she would remember in the morning but when first light came she scarcely even reconsidered. She also had the sense in the night of a clock ticking in double time – there it was, she saw, when she opened her eyes now, the small bronze-faced mantelpiece clock by the china bull – and of a fuzzy light coming from somewhere in the room. She only remembered the light much later, when she realised she was still groggy and decided to take a look at the moat and gardens to clear her head.

She walked out across the lawn with her mobile, hoping for enough signal to call Fran and discuss the phone situation. If she got through she would finish on a casual question as to whether it was OK to have a visitor stay. But as soon as she looked at the screen she noticed a message that made her stop dead, the external world shrinking away into harsh, quiet light.

It was a text from her mum.

Her fingers fumbled quickly across the skin of glass, trying to unlock it and failing. Shaking herself, she keyed in the PIN and then opened the message.

*HeLL swEEt*

What the…?

Hell sweet? Who had got hold of her mum's phone? When had her mum last used it? What a strange, horrible message.

She needed to... She grabbed her hair and looked around at the lawn, the moss-stained path at one edge, a seat, pollarded trees on a bank. There was a bird cawing. She...

Hold on. Her mum hadn't used this for over six months *before* she died. A carer from the local authority, Janet, a lovely woman with a passion for a card game called Uno that she wanted everyone to play with her – she, Janet, had been the last one to use her mum's phone. She had called or texted Alice every day she couldn't come to see her mum in person.

Then what had happened to the phone?

Alice didn't know, she couldn't remember having ever dealt with it after her mum died. She was sure she hadn't seen it again. Why was her memory such a sieve?

Had Janet taken it? Was this an accidental text, sent because the lock screen hadn't activated and it had rubbed against the inside of Janet's – or more likely someone else, a stranger's – pocket?

Alice found the world around her coming back into focus. The sense of unreality was vanishing. There was a practical explanation. It was nothing to get jumpy about. Just a physical accident, a minor, random hiccup in the real world.

She remembered the fuzziness, the strange brightness, in her room in the middle of the night. It was probably the phone at her bedside, kicking into life as the text arrived. Some drunk teenager letting the cheap mobile she'd got off eBay slip out of her hand as she fumbled with her boyfriend, a random number selected as she squirmed on the screen, a random set of letters sent on its journey into space…

Hell sweet.

What a message.

Sweet hell.

How could she have been so lackadaisical about dealing with her mum's phone? It should have been wiped and sent to an African charity. As her mum hadn't used it in years, it must have been so low down on Alice's list of priorities when she died that it hadn't even occurred to her. Had Janet sold it?

She squirmed to think of all the private stuff that might be on there, now in the hands of a stranger. But then again, thinking about it, what was there really? They had no other close relatives, besides a distant Uncle, Bob, in Australia, with his family of sports-loving teenage children. Her mum was a very private person, with only one or two friends, and they had petered out of her life as the Alzheimer's took its increasingly slick grip on her world. Leaving a text history of mundane contact with her daughter as the only significant personal trace.

Should she call the number to let the new owner know what had happened?

No. Let it be. There was nothing on the phone that was too personal.

Something like that would never happen again.


12


The phone was oscillating between one and two bars. It went straight to Fran's answerphone.

'Bloody useless,' Alice cursed.

She typed a short text to her boss about the lack of phones. Matthew's visit would have to wait for a proper conversation.

At the end of the lawn Alice came to the feeder lake, a still green pool with a fair deal of lily and a lot of overgrown scrub. Several mature trees grew on the banks of the lake, including a particularly large beech tree with a number of splintered branches. One of its smooth limbs must at some stage have hung right out over the lake, but it had snapped off, probably in a gale.

Looking around the edges of the water she noticed the pink flowers of Himalayan Balsam, rioting around one corner. She would have to get specialists in to get rid of that, but maybe she could have George cut it back a little in the meantime. If she could find him. She wondered what the protocol was about asking him to do things. She assumed it was all a matter of using the *excellent interpersonal skills* that her CV had assured them she had.

She was curious to walk the boundaries today, to discover the full extent of the grounds. She headed up a steep and decidedly slippery path through the trees at the back of the lake. The woods were bigger than she realised, all bare, black and grey, stricken with fallen branches. You could make a nice extended walk through here, she thought. She'd need a contractor with a digger to put in some safe steps, and possibly to find some shallow gradients to scrape for a disabled route. It was too much to expect volunteers to do.

At one stage as she climbed through the trees she heard a great woody groan, a large, possibly unstable branch, shifting in the breeze. She thought about the broken limb of the beech tree over the lake. How well managed was this wood? Probably not at all, with only George on his own. She would have to get a contractor to make a safety check before opening. Didn't want one of the first visitors to be struck by a falling branch...

Presently she emerged from the treeline and came to a fenced-off field. For a moment she thought it was empty, but then she spotted its sole denizen lurking off towards the hedged corner on her right. She strolled along the fence towards it.

'Hey there, you're a beauty, aren't you?' she said as she approached the bull.

It was a Hereford, ruddy-brown on the back with milk-white legs and head. It was standing still as she approached, parallel to the fence, and it took a few steps away then back again when she came up alongside it. She saw the fence was topped with an electric line. She wouldn't have got so close otherwise.

It was a beautiful creature. She remembered long drives to visit her grandparents' house in Newcastle, a semi in suburbia, and whilst they were a very remote, old-fashioned pair, the visit was always imbued with great value just because she could sit on a small stool covered in a soft patch of goat's hair. That was exactly what the crown of hair on the front of the bull's head reminded her of now. She longed to rub and tug it, to thrust her fingers in it. And that brown coat, the richness of it, the hint of blood in the colour, all that power beneath it. How much muscle could one creature pack beneath its skin?

She spotted a ring in the bull's nose – cruel surely, but somehow quaint – and then someone shouted.

'Hello!'

It was all one-to-one encounters out here in the country. She turned to see a man, from the wellies and waterproofs evidently the farmer, approaching her along the edge of the field. He must have been on the other side of the hedge as she was coming along the fence.

'Hello,' she said.

A smile, white teeth. A large, crooked face that wasn't handsome, but was impressively weather-beaten, with a hint of ginger stubble. Curly hair fanning out around his ears. Brown, hairy hands, no ring, she noticed, as one came up to shake hers.

'Tom Gauge,' he said. 'You must be the new property manager.'

'Yes,' she said. 'Alice Deaton.'

'Pleased to meet you.'

'You run the tenanted property?'

'That's right. Been here for going on twenty-five years.'

'You've still got a hint of the – let me guess, now – Yorkshire accent?'

'Very good.'

'I went to Uni there.'

'Leeds?'

'No, York – Conservation Studies.'

Tom smiled. 'The dear old Smythe-Johnstone's will have you hard at work soon.'

Alice chuckled. She hadn't expected anyone else to use that expression.

'Shouldn't laugh,' she said, realising she really *shouldn't*. If she was going to build trust she couldn't go laughing at the S-Js behind their back.

'Don't worry,' he said. 'Fran and I know each other well. I'm fully behind the Trust's approach.'

'Will it mean anything different for you? As a tenant?' said Alice. 'I realise I should know but I'm afraid I don't.'

'Not unless you whack the rent up!'

'Oh I don't…'

'No, I know you won't. Fran's been talking it through with me. She even thinks she'll be able to freeze it from inflation if you get the visitor numbers through.'

'Which I'm sure we will.'

'Aye – it's a special place, that's for sure.'

'It is. It really is. I've never seen anything like it. But there's so much to do, I hardly know where to start.'

'Clear all that clutter.'

'Yes – but there's terrible cracks in the ceiling and walls.'

'That's just the plaster. Nothing to worry about with that. That house is built of local ragstone, it'll last forever.'

'That's a relief.'

There was a snort from beside them and they both turned to look at the bull, which was now considering them.

'Saw you admiring Fred here when I came up,' said Tom.

'Yes, he's a fine-looking beast.'

'A prize-winner, no less.'

Alice listened intently as he sketched out the bare bones of his smallholding, which was mainly cattle and dairy, with a few fields of arable down the other side of the hill. If she hadn't decided on Conservation Studies, Agriculture would have been her second choice for a degree – despite there being absolutely no connection between her family and the land in living memory. She just loved the idea of working outdoors, with animals, in all weather.

'I need to be getting on,' he said finally. 'Promised myself I'd make a start on reconciling the wheat crops this lunchtime.'

'Even you farmers don't escape the paperwork,' said Alice.

'At least it's a chance to rest your feet.'

When she reached the break in the trees Alice stopped to take in the splendid view of Bramley below. There were the woods, jumbled brown with bursts of green holly and a bronze under-scatter of leaves, following the protective curve of the hill; the still black drop of the lake, and the green lawn; then the building itself, with its small moat and slate roofs. It was a great spot to take in the full extent of the property. She would have to get a proper path up here, the visitors would love it.

A man and his bull.

She grinned and walked back down into the woods, wondering what it was about older men.

13

She often spotted things other people didn't notice. She was a *details person*, her mum used to say. And now here she was examining faint scratches in the sandstone plinth above the enormous Great Hall fireplace.

The scratches were a series of *V*s and semi-circles, overlapping, the circles sliced in half at the top edge of the fireplace. Her initial thoughts were vandalism, graffiti. Someone had decided to make their mark here. But then, the more she thought about it, the more she thought it was too repetitive for graffiti. When someone wanted to do their equivalent of a little wee to associate their fractional lives with antiquity they usually marked their name or initials. If they were just bored, they might do a picture, often rude. But this was too consistent, too geometrical. And too high for a child.

No, someone had definitely…

She was interrupted by the sound of claws scratching lightly on wood, the murmur of conversation. Soon the black Lab, Henry, came loping into the Hall through the door, followed by Samantha and Bernard S-J.

'Looking at our witch marks?' Bernard called, his voice loud but not quite echoing across the vault of the room.

'Is that what they are?'

She pushed at Henry's jowls whilst the two elderly people came up and stopped in front of her.

'The Vs are for the Virgin, they're hoping for the protection of Mary. The circles leave the old hags with nowhere to hide…'

'Bernard,' said Samantha. 'We don't use that word anymore.'

'No shady corners in a circle you see,' the old man continued, tilting his large forehead slightly to acknowledge his wife's remark. The parting at the top of that forehead was thin but his hair was still a pale strawberry blond. He must be in his late seventies, Alice mused, as her marketing head switched on.

'Are there any stories about witches in the house?' she asked. 'There's that painting up in the Priest's room, too, the old woman suckling the cow.' She could see a good PR opportunity, round Halloween perhaps.

'Every house over a certain age has its tales of witches,' said Samantha.

'And ghosts,' said her husband, his voice catching as if he had a cold.

'How are you settling in?' said Samantha.

'Got a feel for the old place, yet?' said Bernard.

Alice nodded. 'Yes, I've just been up the top of the woods and met Mr Gauge, our tenant.'

She watched Bernard's eyes flick sharply to hers. The *our* had been carefully chosen, part of the drip feed.

'Gauge is a good man,' he said. 'How long have we had him, dear?'

'Nearly twenty-five years,' Alice answered.

'That's right,' said Samantha.

'Was Fred up there?' said Bernard.

'The Hereford? Yes.'

'Gauge breeds some first-rate animals,' said Bernard, then added: 'Sam said you can fix our tapestries.'

'No I didn't!'

'Well…' began Alice.

'Says you're a trained textiles conservator?'

'Yes, but whilst looking after the collection is obviously paramount, textile conservation is not strictly what I came here to do…'

'Come on, come with me. Come and have a look at it.'

Alice realised he was an old charmer, used to getting his way.

'Bernard, you're incorrigible! Not now…'

'No, I don't mind. I'd love to have a look at it,' said Alice.

'Sick!' said Bernard.

'What?'

'That's what you kids say today, isn't it? Means good.'

'I'm twenty-seven.'

'He doesn't mean to be such an oaf,' said Samantha.

Whilst Samantha took Henry off for his afternoon walk, Alice followed Bernard back through the house. He took her down the south wing, along the hall that passed the kitchen and dining room and through the long, partitioned library. As they walked he pointed things out to her.

'That's a Geeraerts, Dutch painter,' he said, pointing offhandedly to a portrait of a ginger-haired lady with a ruff in the corridor. 'And that's one of Churchill's watercolours of Bramley...'

'Winston?' said Alice.

'Yes, he stayed here a few times. They say he got the idea for the eighteenth-century doorcase he had his architect put in at Chartwell here. That's an Albarello vase, Middle Eastern medicine thing, and over there's...'

Alice walked along behind him as if in a dream. This was the first time she'd had the house's collection vividly brought to life for her. Bernard was clearly the one with the passion for the art and objects. She just wished he would slow down.

'... love this sideboard here, never know the exact date, clearly Elizabethan, there's the Queen herself, look at all that hair, fabulous, little ceramic chap with a broken leg here, think he's Greek.' Towards the end of the corridor he stopped and turned abruptly to face her in the dim light. She noticed for the first time that he was not a tall man, barely an inch or so taller than her.

'Are you interested in all this stuff?' he asked. His eyebrows did that funny thing she'd noticed at the interview, lifting and dropping from left to right like a caterpillar.

'Yes. Yes, very,' she said.

'Good,' he said. 'People will say anything to get a damned job these days.'

'You sound like you have hard-earned experience,' she said, as he turned and led her on into the large Squire's room, the last room at the end of the hall.

'Just your predecessor,' he said.

'Didn't she care for the collection?'

'Oh, she said the right stuff at first. In interview. But as soon as she was in, she showed herself to be a right bossy little madam. Just wanted to get on and run the show without us.'

Alice felt her cheeks burn but remained composed as she followed him into the room.

'But Bramley will always be ours, regardless of a few scraps of paper. Our family has been here for nearly three hundred years, looking after this place. It is – I was going to say it's ours – but no, it's more than ours. It's England's. In some way it is England. Old England, England right from the time of the peasant archers at Agincourt, to Drake's defeat of the Armada, Churchill's trouncing of the Nazis. It's always been here, it's deep and... am I going on a bit?'

Alice breathed out loudly through her nose, surprised at his change of tone.

'No,' she said. 'And of course, you're right. Bramley is England's. And that's exactly what the Trust for England is here to do. Preserve what is England's. For the English.'

44

'And our visitors from the continent and across the pond, of course,' said Bernard. 'And those Orientals too, lots of them coming over these days.'

'Yes.'

Did that go well? She couldn't say. It was a nightmare discussing England and its place in the world these days.

Bernard was now standing over by the northern wall, the one furthest from the two tall, bright windows on the western wall and the single, smaller window on the eastern, courtyard wall. She went over to him.

Here was the tapestry.

It was a small hanging, about the size of a family dinner table. It depicted a man in classical garb assaulting a bull. He was aided by a group of animals and watched by a figure in the corner with yellow spikes jutting from his helmet, clearly a representation of the sun. The man was plunging a dagger into the bull's chest, whilst the animals all helped to bring the creature down – a raven by pecking its back, a snake and dog by biting its throat, and a scorpion by stinging it – she frowned, and peered closer – yes, the scorpion was definitely striking the bull's scrotum.

'What do you think?'

'Well, it's a good piece,' she said, her eyes quickly scanning the colours, the detail of the warp and weft, the state of the fabric. 'Wool with silk. Victorian, with their love for a good classic Greco-Roman scene. There's some damage to the fibres, but it's good quality and there's no holes, which is great. Silk normally shows a lot more damage than this, someone's looked after it. Do you know how the stain happened?'

In the bottom left there was a deep purplish blotch, covering most of the bull's forelegs.

'Red wine,' he said.

'Oh. Someone must have put it on the floor at some stage. How dreadful.' She hoped for a moment it hadn't been him, but the way he continued reassured her it wasn't.

'Is there anything you can do about it?' he said.

'Me? No, not on my own. It would need to go to a lab. The Trust will have one, or at least have an arrangement with someone. I can find out for you.'

'Oh, that'll take ages, all that form filling and stuff, sending it off for months or years. It's one of my favourites. How would you go about doing it on your own, without a lab?'

Alice looked at him. The tapestry clearly meant a lot to him, it might be a good way to build trust.

'Well, you have to wash it first, in demineralised water. Then I'd dry it using a towel and a roll of plastic to keep the pressure even. Then I'd check for bleeds, but I guess this has... not been cleaned for a long time, so there's not much bleeding. For the stain, well... you're going to have to see how it looks after the wash. I'd probably wash it again with a conservation grade detergent. Wash and check, wash and check again. That's the idea.'

'Do you think you could try it?'

'I'd want to send it to the lab first. I'd lose my job if I went ahead and did it myself! You don't have the right facilities here. This has heritage value.'

'Heritage value,' repeated Bernard, quietly. Alice suspected he was mocking her. If he was, he was clearly trying to hide it.

Suddenly Bernard's eyes lit up. 'How about if you ask Fran?' he said. 'She could give you permission, surely?'

'I'll speak to her about it.'

'Good girl!'

Good girl? Really? How was he going to feel when she set up her first school visit with a group of hardcore teenagers from a Telford comp?

## 14

Alice spent the rest of the afternoon in between the Squire's room and the Great Hall, starting a handwritten inventory of objects, guessing at countries and periods, and recording state of repair. She began to feel increasingly frustrated, she was unsure of so much. She didn't even know if the collection belonged to the Trust now or whether it remained in the ownership of the S-Js. At least she'd had a text from Fran, saying she would be with her next day. She had a hundred questions to ask her.

But the truth was, as she sat beneath the giant windows of the Great Hall, gazing at a model of a manor house in a glass dome, her mind was starting to drift. It was the text message from her mum's phone that had got to her. The other oddities, the brief impression of the boy in the hood and the witch symbols – had washed over her, all part and parcel of her vivid, no *hyperactive*, imagination coming into contact with this ancient place. But the message from her mum was somehow... cruel, in a way she couldn't specify.

*HeLL swEEt.* This job was her once-in-a-lifetime opportunity, her break with the miseries of the past. Why did fate have to go and bamboozle her with such a leftfielder? Of course it was just an accident, one of the random outcomes of new technology but... after all she'd been through, losing her dad in an accident when she was twelve, then her mum's dementia, it just didn't seem fair.

Life doesn't owe you a living, Deaton.

But peering at the small coterie of plastic visitors to the model house – the painted country gentleman in top hat, his wife, daughter and white spaniel dog – she knew it had kindled something she thought quashed years ago. A particularly teenage anxiety, a fear not just of the outside world, of having to eternally interact with all those people with their arbitrary habits – but also a larger fear, of her own mind and thoughts. Of existence itself, and what she might, under certain circumstances, think and do. Of what she might become. It was a strange fear, a fear which ultimately resided in anxiety, or worse, insanity.

For a girl who loved to be alone it was the deepest kind of betrayal, to have her solitude invaded by a terror from within.

She had done the work herself, trained the fear out of her mind. Every time doubt began to put out its black feelers, she shut it down. Did something else, or if she was shut up somewhere, encased in an aeroplane, she thought about something else. Thought hard. And eventually, after the best part of a year, and after what she now thought of as *the intervention*, the feeling and all its dark, accompanying thoughts – had gone.

But now, looking at the red lips of the gentleman's daughter, her tiny, black-dot eyes, she remembered it again.

## 15

And so it was the first thing on her mind when she awoke in the middle of that night.

The terror.

A mass of dark, eyeless vipers, striking, seething, writhing through the shallows of her mind.

She fumbled across the bedside table for her phone, needing artificial light. Momentarily, she felt it slip against the edge of her palm, she'd failed to grab it, there was a clunk as the phone hit the floor. She propped herself up on an elbow.

Then realised she was not alone.

The room was black, almost pitch black, despite the fact she hadn't bothered to draw the curtains. But no matter how dark a space, you can always tell when someone is in a room with you.

Someone a few paces away, standing near the fireplace. Wasn't there?

Her heart felt like someone was squeezing it, quick as they could. Like her mum's balloon pump, when the group for her little daughter's party arrived early.

'Who's there?' she said.

She felt a rustle, a movement in the air, like the shift of a chiffon gown on the floor.

Slowly, steadily, keeping her eyes fixed on the place she knew the mantelpiece to be, she reached down to feel for her phone on the floor.

Had one of the S-Js come into her room? Had she locked the door? Was Samantha, or worse still, Bernard, standing there, watching her in bed? What would they do that for? Oh God, no…

There was noise as the phone scraped along the floor. Immediately she grabbed it, awkwardly but firmly enough to lift it. Then she was shaking it, no, the wrong end, it wouldn't work that way, turning it, fumbling, shaking it again.

The fierce little light broke the room's night.

Alice shrieked.

There was a woman standing in her room. She was wearing a dark patterned dress. Her hair, her eyes, were dark too. She was watching Alice in her bed.

Alice felt her skin moving, all over her body. Her mouth was dry.

'What do you want?'

Slowly, the woman shook her head, her long hair coming forward over her shoulders. She put her hands together in front of her and began to fidget them.

'What do you want?' Alice sat up in bed, jerking the torchlight back up to keep it on the woman.

The woman's eyebrows began to move, creasing down, her mouth twitched, her shoulders lifted and dropped.

'Say something,' said Alice.

The woman glanced sideways, towards the door, and then horror shook Alice as she began to step towards her bed. She opened her mouth, saying something – but no sound came out. Alice noticed she had particularly large teeth, a gap in the middle. And her flowery dress was cut just below the knee, in a contemporary style.

'Stay back, please,' she said.

The woman's eyes were the darkest Alice had ever seen, dark like a South American's. They transfixed her. They were liquid, full of sensation. Alice felt it. She felt it.

'What?' she muttered, as the woman bore down on her, all the time fidgeting with her hands.

Now she was only a couple of steps away from her and Alice shifted backwards, right up against the headboard of the bed. Fleetingly she wondered whether this was an intruder, some mad woman come in from the night. Maybe she had a knife? Had she been locked away in the house, kept in a basement by the S-Js? But her mind was leading her towards something else, trying fast to process, refuting entirely the possibility that this could be a dream, prompting a buried memory, a…

Suddenly, the figure lunged forward. Alice shrieked as the woman lifted up a hand and thrust the palm at her face. Alice just had time to make out a swollen red lump, a small gash on the palm, before she dropped her phone again, face up on the quilt so the torchlight vanished, leaving the room once more in total darkness.

She picked the phone up in an instant, swung the silver beam around the bedroom.

For a moment she thought the woman had gone, she wasn't near the fire, the door, the tapestry… But then, as she swung the beam around past the small door of the garderobe, she jumped as she saw her again, standing at the window beside the bed, just a couple of feet away from her. But now she wasn't looking at Alice, she was peering out of the window and down, down across the lawn towards the woods and lake.

'What are you doing?' said Alice.

The woman turned towards her and Alice saw that her face was crumpled, on the verge of tears. She felt a tide of sadness sweep over her.

'What is it?' said Alice again.

The woman turned back to the window, then vanished head-first through it.

16

The thing was, she wasn't afraid of ghosts.

The violence of humankind and nature, the ridiculous enormity of outer space, the fragile skin of existence, the unfathomable mystery of the origins of life and thought – all these things could petrify her, if she allowed them. But ghosts? No.

Alice wasn't scared of ghosts for a very good reason. She had met (experienced?) them before, and they had never hurt her. They always seemed to have a purpose, and one had even transformed her life.

As she sat there now in that bed, in the middle of the still, quiet night with the lights on, she was remembering the other times.

The first was when she was very small. She wasn't good at recalling how old she had been when things happened, her childhood was mostly a mix of camera shots combined with kaleidoscopic feelings for people, places and repeat activities such as holidays with grandparents.

There were, however, some pointed exceptions, most explicit of which was her first meeting with a ghost. Of course, at the time she had never realised it was a ghost. She was sitting on his lap in the lounge and they were reading a story together. She couldn't remember the book, it was a proper reading book but it did have cartoonish pictures, and he was speaking to her. His mouth was close to her ear, so close it was ticklish.

52

She couldn't recall a single word the man said to her, that little girl sitting on his lap in a red and orangey coloured room, the late afternoon sun aglow through wooden blinds. But after her dad came in, bright and whistling, and the book dropped back down suddenly on to the leather sofa, she remembered how he had made her *feel*.

Safe. Safe, and aware of something that had a special value. Something she could never define, and never deny.

She had not experienced another until her fifteenth birthday. That was towards the end of the period she had remembered earlier in the Great Hall, the time when she had first known that dwarfing, existential fear. Her dad had died three years earlier, a sudden and senseless death after he ventured out onto a tiny bluff on the Welsh coast and was literally blown off by the wind. The manner of his death would have suggested suicide if there hadn't been another pair of walkers out that day, a middle-aged couple from Pontypool, who saw him with his camera heading dangerously close to the edge for a shot – and then, with a sudden gust, stumbling, vanishing. And besides, she knew her dad, he was too sanguine to take his own life.

Her dad's death may have been the seed to the development of that fear; she would never know. But develop it did, two years later, becoming something that genuinely threatened to send her off the rails – in a quiet, Alice-kind of way. She had tried to keep it to herself but eventually had to tell her mum, who had done everything she could, including plenty of suggestions for new activities and breaks away (could taking up crochet or a weekend in Eastbourne really help her angst?), a visit to the local priest, and plenty of hugs. But it just got worse and worse, until she found a website *wellteenonline* and began to take seriously some of the practical techniques, experiences, and values shared there. She read some books that the website recommended and found herself able to gradually – very gradually – turn things around. After a few months she was going through whole mornings without a shadowy thought or panic attack.

But then there was Susannah Pugh at school, a persistent bully who unlike most other bullies operated almost entirely alone. Later, it made Alice wonder if she was perhaps a psychopath. For a few months it had seemed like they were becoming good friends, they both had an interest in art and particularly the classics, which made them pretty unique at St Peter's school. But then, something changed in Susannah and she began to undermine Alice wherever and whenever she could. (Alice always wished she could have at least known what it was she'd done to make Susannah mad, it might have made the next six months more bearable, or at least understandable). At first she started with small things – not turning up at an arranged meeting place or showing sudden, uncharacteristic disinterest in a new book or idea that Alice was keen on and thought she would like. But when Alice began to despair about her reliability and started to make friends with a plain but kind girl, Charlotte Hemingway, Susannah suddenly turned nasty and began to undermine her in more serious ways. First she told Alice's favourite teacher, Joanna Long, who taught Alice music in a lunchtime class, that Alice was smoking at school. It was a complete lie, but Joanna had to inform the Headteacher and investigate it. Despite assuring Alice they believed her, it nevertheless left an awkward atmosphere between all three of them.

Then one day Alice and Charlotte came into class together and Alice noticed two girls at the back, neither of them the usual suspects, glancing at them, whispering and laughing. Soon they came to realise that there was a rumour circulating they were lesbians. Alice knew who had started it. She felt angry and helpless. Angry because it wasn't true; and helpless because she thought denial would show her up to be prejudiced against gay people, which went against everything she believed in.

It was a particularly cruel rumour, based on Susannah's deep knowledge of her values and feelings. And it set Alice's progress on her anxiety back to square one. The agoraphobia and panic attacks returned.

Her mum became very worried about her. When Alice admitted the trigger to her – Susannah's betrayal – her mum took it up persistently with the Headteacher. Mr Stanton did his best to resolve the situation but his efforts were hampered by just how charming and deceitful Susannah could be. Alice began to lose her appetite and weight. Susannah eased off for a while, but she knew she would be back at her when the adult attention had subsided.

Then *the intervention* happened.

It was her fifteenth birthday. She was walking home from school, down the railway embankment, on a damp, blustery autumn day. There was nothing special planned for the day besides Charlotte coming round for a pizza and carrot cake prepared by her mum, followed by watching a movie together. Somehow Susannah, who followed Alice's route home along the embankment before she turned off to Farnborough Green, was with them. In the odd way of teenagers, they were talking as if the last six months had never happened. But Alice was aching inside.

They had just reached the underpass, a graffitied concrete tunnel surrounded by brambles filled with poop bags and crisp packets, when a woman appeared, coming towards them from a side path. She was old, and wet from the rain. Her short, grey hair was stuck to her head. She was dressed completely inappropriately, in what looked like a white dressing gown.

'Who's that?' said Susannah.

For a moment Alice couldn't take her eyes of the woman, she had a strange, fixed look on her face and was coming towards them like a… like a zombie, or something. But then she noticed Charlotte, who was standing absolutely rigid, staring at the woman, mouth open.

'What is it?' she asked.

'It's my gran,' replied Charlotte, barely audible in the wind.

'Oh,' said Alice. 'What's she doing out –'

'She died last year,' said Charlotte, so quietly Alice was not sure she had heard right.

She looked back at the old woman, who was almost upon them now. Her cheeks were scored by deep, vertical wrinkles and her mouth sagged open revealing pasty grey teeth. She looked really sick. But her sad, rheumy eyes, strewn with rainwater, remained fixed on one person.

Susannah.

'What do you want?' said Susannah as the woman strode towards her. Then, more urgently, she shrieked 'Get away!' She thrust up a hand to protect herself.

Briefly, before the old woman – the ghost – did what she did, she passed a brief, complicit glance at Alice and Charlotte.

Then she became a frenzied mess of light, spark and strangeness, slicing in and wrapping round Susannah all at once. During the whole process – which felt like it lasted for ages as an observer, but which probably only took a second or two – the girl screamed, gasped, cried and wailed, shaking herself ineffectually, because after all, how do you keep a ghost off?

And then the ghost, Charlotte's gran, was gone.

The effect on Susannah Pugh was brutal. She completely withdrew from everyone and never spoke to Alice or Charlotte again. The next year her parents moved her away to a private school, fearing for her health.

Only the three of them ever knew the truth.


17


Her final experience of a ghost – excluding this evening's one, of course – was a far more nebulous affair, soon after her mum had passed away.

She had been thrown – yet again – into a pit of despair, and was wondering how she would cope. This time she was on her own. She had a few friends, mainly from work, but there was no one close to her. Her friendship with Charlotte had strengthened after the Susannah incident, but then she'd got married to a German businessman and was now living in Geneva with three children. They never talked.

For several weeks she had struggled to get on top of her grief, forcing herself to go through the ropes at Albany Park. Then, one night, sitting up late in front of a switched-off TV, when the crying was so bad it was crushing the air from her lungs, she'd felt a presence.

This time, she didn't see anything. Instead, it felt like there was something inside her, behind her eyes. Something trying to push through a membrane that was thin, stretching, but ultimately tough, unbreakable. She remembered the things she'd felt in the presence of the other ghosts. She began to speak to the entity, saying who knows what, talking fast, possibly even randomly, talking *in tongues* as the Christians would say. Afterwards, she would have the bizarre feeling that through her words she had been trying to give birth to the creature.

Finally, talking all the time (the neighbours through the paper-thin walls would think she was drunk), she had picked up a pen and, in capital letters, written down just one word on a post-it note by the phone.

HOPE.

## 18

Now, sitting on the bed, she began to reconsider her experiences at Bramley.

The boy in the burgundy hood. Surely a ghost. Where was he running? The priest's room or the chapel? Or down those stairs? The text from her mum? Was someone trying to communicate with her? Surely not her mum herself? Perhaps it was. She hoped *hell sweet* didn't mean her mum was suffering in the afterlife. Sweet hell. Maybe the old-fashioned Christians were exactly right, and hell was real? But why would her mum end up there? She thought about horror books and films, where evil entities masqueraded as loved ones…

Then she remembered something, the last Christmas card her mum had sent her. With its simple picture of a robin on the holly, and no special message, Alice suspected it was one that Janet had got for her. It was probably a freebie, given to encourage you to donate to charity at Christmas. But her mum had written in it, in the new shaky handwriting that looked nothing like her old, tiny script, and it was an unusual message for her.

*I love u – sweethart.*

She'd never called her that before.

Maybe the text wasn't finished.

Hello sweetheart.

It was a possibility.

But it was all so much to process – without even starting on the young woman who had just appeared in her room.

Alice checked the door, turned off the light, and fumbled her way back into bed.

It was a long time before her mind slowed, before she slept.


19

'All I can say is, I am very, very impressed.'

Fran looked up from Alice's notebook and smiled. 'Some of the things here, like the one-way flow system through the house, I'd already been thinking – but the idea of the café in the crypt – genius!'

'There's nothing you'd lose by doing it,' said Alice excitedly. 'No need to move anything around, no threat to the collection, or anything.'

'And right by the kitchen,' said Fran.

'Of course, we'd need to open a proper one at a later date, something purpose built. This place is going to be popular.'

Fran nodded. 'I knew we'd picked the right one in you,' she said. She sloshed coffee from the cafetière into both cups, then took another of the chocolate cookies she'd brought with her and chomped into it.

'And how are you getting along with the Smythe-Johnstones?'

'Fine,' said Alice. Then added: '*Ish.*'

Fran cocked an eyebrow. 'Not causing you trouble, are they?'

'No, not at all. I've not seen as much of them as I expected. Samantha was very frank about the situation when I met her. I think she's adjusted. I'm not so sure about Bernard.'

'Yes, Bernard's the one. Samantha is in control of a lot of stuff on the surface, the day-to-day stuff – but Bernard has… What would you call it?'

'The passion.'

'Yes, that's as good a word as any. He's got the passion for the place. It's in his blood.'

'Hardly surprising. I've only been here a few days and I'm starting to feel it myself.'

'Yes. Imagine what it would be like if you'd lived here all your life – and your ancestors before you.'

'He's asked me to ask you something,' said Alice.

'Yes?'

'He's got this old tapestry in the Squire's room, it's not in too bad condition generally but it's got a stain.'

'The Mithras one?'

'Mithras?' Alice had heard the name, but struggled to recall who it was.

'The one with the bull getting it from all sides.'

'That's it. Remind me who or what Mithras was again?'

'One of the ancient Roman mystery religions. It spread all over the Empire but was almost completely wiped out by Christianity.'

'Yep, I remember it now from my classics lessons at school. Bernard wants me to try and clean it up, remove the stain. I said it should be done in a lab – I assume we have a contractor who does those things – but he didn't seem to want it sent away. He suggested I ask you if I could do it. I wouldn't normally, but I think it might be a way to build some goodwill.'

'What period?'

'Victorian.'

'I agree. You are trained in that kind of thing, so I think we can risk it.'

'OK, I'll do my best.'

'Great – shall we take a look at that woodwork in the Great Hall now?'

Alice was amazed at how quickly Fran had demolished her third cookie, when she was still only halfway through her first.

'Yes,' she said, taking a quick bite of the biscuit and putting it back on the plate.

# 20

In the Great Hall, Alice showed the Regional Manager the window ledge where she thought there might be dry rot.

Fran bent down close to smell.

'Yes, I think so,' she said.

'I'm no expert on it, but I remember my Uncle Bob when he was over, he identified some in our garage just by the smell,' said Alice.

'Over from where?' said Fran.

'Australia.'

'Wow, what a great place to have relatives. Or *rellys*, as they say over there,' said Fran, standing and smiling closely into Alice's face. 'Bet you've taken advantage of that a few times, had a few trips over?'

'No,' said Alice. 'Unfortunately not. He came over here once when I was a girl, though.'

'Well, can't imagine you'll get a chance for a holiday soon, but once we're opened you should make the effort.'

'I can't see it,' said Alice, shrugging. 'We don't have anything to do with each other now. Have you been?'

'Me? No.'

After a moment's silence, Alice said: 'There's another thing I wanted to show you in here.'

She led Fran over to the fireplace and pointed out the circles and *V*s. The large woman leaned forward and peered at them.

'Some kind of ward? Doesn't look like your average run-of-the-mill graffiti,' she said.

'Yes. Bernard said it's to keep the witches away.'

'Interesting,' said Fran, straightening. 'And a perfect hook for the visitors. You've got to have spookiness in a place like this, the customers positively demand it!'

'Are there any stories of Bramley being haunted?' Alice tried to deliver it as levelly as she could, despite the fact her lungs suddenly felt like they had emptied of air.

Fran rubbed her finger across the scratches – surprising Alice, because surely that wasn't good practice? – and said: 'Not that I've heard of. I'm sure there are some. We'll have to pick the *dear olds'* brains.'

She looked round keenly at Alice again. 'Why? You've not been hearing things go bump in the night?'

She sounded her usual rambunctious self, but was there a hint of apprehension in her eyes? Alice shook her head.

'No,' she said.


21


After lunch, they walked around the grounds. Alice wanted to show Fran the possible route she thought they should put in through the woods to the top field. George was sitting on an ancient-looking mower, cutting the main lawn. He waved cheerfully at them as they walked up to him. The roar of the petrol engine subsided into a wobbly splutter as Fran called:

'Final one of the season, is it?'

George nodded and lifted a thumb.

'You've met Alice already, she tells me?'

He nodded again and grinned at Alice.

'She's your new boss, now,' said Fran.

George dipped his black curly fringe at them. Then, sitting back in the seat of the old juddering machine, he pointed a thumb at his chest. He made the shape of a heart with his fingers, followed by a *T*, four fingers, and something that took Alice a moment to realise was an *E*.

Alice smiled and glanced at Fran, who was looking up at George with a mischievous grin on her face.

'Yes, we all love the Trust for England, Jerry,' said Fran.

As soon as they were on their way again, heading up past the lake towards the woods with the noise of the mower abating, Alice said: 'Why did you call him Jerry?'

'Did I?' said Fran. 'Oops. That was the name of the other gardener. Similar age, but a bit more… *experienced* – left a few months ago. How embarrassing. Senior moment.'

'You can't be a day over thirty-five.'

'Flattery will get you everywhere.'

'Have you managed to get me on to the Induction Training yet like you promised?' said Alice.

'I have,' said Fran and paused.

'I can sense a *but*.'

'I'm afraid there wasn't one free until December – December 14th. I thought of sending you off to another region but half the point of these courses is to meet your fellow co-workers. Start building some relationships face-to-face.'

'Yes, I totally agree about meeting other staff from the region,' said Alice. 'I'm happy to wait, it's only a couple of months.'

'On another note, I have been successful in getting you someone to help with the cataloguing,' said Fran.

'Excellent!' said Alice. 'Who?'

'His name is David Bridge, he's one of our National Committee members and he's a Professor of Art History with specialism in the Elizabethan period.'

'Is the National Committee the same as the Board?'

'No – the Committee appoints the Board, and it's larger. The members advise the board on strategy, and keep the Board connected to members and local issues. They're all very passionate about what they do. I had a word with David about Bramley – and you – the other day and he said he'd love to help you out for a day or two with the cataloguing.'

'Sounds great.'

'It is – and a real boon, as he's free!'

'Save the Trust some cash,' said Alice.

'Ex-bloody-actly!' Fran exclaimed, chuckling.

Alice was starting to realize that, at least half of the time, saving money was what it was all about.


## 22

They walked on for a while, again discussing the urgent need for the IT infrastructure in Bramley. Fran told Alice that Regional Office had sent out the request for quotes for broadband installation now.

'It won't be long,' she said. 'I know it's a nightmare for you.'

'Well yes, it makes things very difficult,' said Alice. 'There's lots of things I can't do without proper internet access and email. I can do some of it on my phone, when the connection is OK…'

'But you shouldn't be having to,' said Fran. 'I can only apologise.'

'How did the other girl do it?'

'Jenny? She was only here for a short time.'

'Did she make any progress – with anything?'

'No. As I say, she was hopeless. Timid and bossy at the same time. In the end, she told me that it just didn't suit her out here. You know, you've got to believe in something like this to do the hours and – *cope* – with the unusual living conditions.'

Alice wanted to ask more, but she could sense a reluctance in Fran to talk about her predecessor. She would save that for another time, if ever. Now she had something else to request, and the discussion around the living environment provided her with the ideal opening.

'Yes,' she said. 'There's something I just wanted to check with you. Check that it's OK.'

Ahead, there was a sudden bashing of undergrowth that made them both jump. A dark lump rose up out of the brambles and began to stream away in between the grey trees.

'Bloody grouse,' said Fran.

'I've invited my boyfriend to come and stay for a weekend,' said Alice.

'What?'

'My boyfriend, Matthew.'

Fran watched the bird disappearing into the autumnal murk.

'I'm surprised the Smythe-Johnstone's didn't ask you about that in the interview,' she said, once the grouse had gone.

'They did,' said Alice.

'Oh, so you told them about it.'

'No. It's only been going on for a few weeks.'

'A work colleague seizing his – or her – final chance?'

Alice flushed. 'Yes. As a matter of fact… yes. He did.' She felt awkward. Fran should feel awkward.

'No, that's fine,' said Fran, brusquely. 'It'll give them – the *dear olds* – something to chew on…'

## 23

Later, after cleaning the kitchen floor, Alice lay the tapestry out on the flagstones.

In one of her cataloguing sessions she had discovered a container of demineralised water in the Butler's pantry. Someone had obviously bought some for the ironing, or perhaps for some textile cleaning of their own in the past. She decided that she would give it a go there and then. She would see how the water did on its own. If she needed a chemical detergent, she would have to get Fran to order some for her.

She studied the picture under the bright neon light, supplemented by a reading lamp she'd brought in from the library.

The centrepiece was a man, Mithras evidently, wearing one of those curved, Phrygian caps. *Noddy* caps, as she liked to think of them. He was kneeling on the clearly exhausted bull, gripping its nostrils with his left hand, and stabbing it with his right. As he did so, he was looking over his shoulder towards the Sun god in the corner. Around the bull, the dog leapt up and bit at its throat, whilst the snake struck just below the wound of Mithras' blade. At the bottom, the scorpion seemed to be fully clamped on to the poor creature's genitals.

Beside the god were two torchbearers and, at either edge of the panel, two giant pillar-like figures, caryatidstyle men, holding keys as they were being constricted by giant snakes. They had beards and tiny wings on their shoulders.

'You poor, poor creature...' she muttered to the bull, as she set to work.

It took her nearly three hours to carefully wash the whole tapestry, using the water and a full set of new cloths. She hadn't done any textile conservation work for several years and had almost forgotten how much she enjoyed it. She went into a kind of satisfied trance, completely unaware of the passage of time. It was a state that enabled her to think very freely, with a valuable sense of perspective.

Ghosts in Bramley... why hadn't she shared her experience with Fran in the end? She had been fluctuating about it right up until the RM drove off in her battered old Ford. Alice might not be scared of ghosts *per se* – but that encounter with the woman in the floral dress had been pretty hardcore. It had loomed over her thoughts all day, not least because she wondered whether she was going to be visiting her again tonight. And the night after? That's the trouble with ghosts, you just didn't know when they were going to turn up. She wasn't sure how her nerves would take it.

The woman was a fretful, nervous character. That was clear. The way she'd fidgeted with her hands in front of her, it was as if she was worried about showing Alice something. Her wound, of course. What was that welt, that blister with a gash, on the palm of her right hand? It was a strange kind of wound. Alice was reminded of a horrible story someone had once told her, an urban myth no doubt, about a woman who had gone on holiday and been bitten on the neck by a spider. The bite swelled up when she got back home, then burst and lots of baby spiders came running out. She still squirmed to think of that story. What could have made that kind of injury on the woman's hand? Could it be a bite of some kind?

And what was with the disappearance at the window? It was as if the woman had hurled herself out. Was she a suicide?

And again… why hadn't she told Fran? For the same reason she hadn't told the S-Js, of course. Professional pride. She could just imagine Bernard's turn of phrase behind closed doors. *Hysterical young madam.* We've got another one here. Or something like that.

She would keep it to herself. For as long as she could.

Now, as she dabbed away at the wool and silk of the tapestry, she noticed there was something about the pillar-guys at the edges… She peered more closely at them. They had curious ridges on their foreheads, jutting jaws, and their eyes had kinks at the corners. Catlike kinks. Then, *Lions*, she thought. They've got lion heads. This Mithras cult certainly liked its symbols. She would have to look it up. *Next time she had access to the bloody web.*

She eased herself up, feeling the pain in her knees and back from being on all fours too long. She needed to stretch her legs so headed out into the corridor, and down towards the library. As she passed a window looking out over the courtyard, she noticed a trail of smoke coming from one of the chimneys. She looked back at the corridor, intending to carry on – and then stopped and looked again.

The S-Js had lit their fire!

It must be theirs, it was the chimney stack right above their wing.

She turned and headed up the nearby stairs, which brought her out right in front of their quarters.

She knocked on the door marked *Private*.

There was a low rumbling sound behind the door, followed by a thump, and then a bang. A moment later the door opened to reveal Samantha, her brown hair frizzy, unbrushed.

'Hello, Alice,' she said.

'Hello Samantha,' said Alice. 'I hope you're well. I just noticed that there's smoke coming out of your chimney.'

'Yes, Bernard was feeling the cold so we lit the fire. This old central heating system is…'

'You know that's not allowed. It's Trust policy. No fires in the building.'

'What?'

'It sounds like you didn't realise?'

'I've never heard anything so ridiculous. We always have fires in the winter. It's cold.'

'But it was –' Alice began, before she realised she hadn't seen them, so couldn't say for certain, '– it *should* have been in the documents you received.' And Fran should have told you, she thought.

'Oh, we're old, we don't have time to read all of those,' said the woman. Her lips twitched a little.

'Well, it's part of the agreement.'

'But we'll catch our deaths in this weather.'

Alice paused, thinking. She noticed Bernard appear, he had been doing something in the part of the room that was out of her line of sight.

'Look, I'm sure we can get the system serviced or, if not, I think we might be able to get a new one put in. The Trust will need to make sure it's warm enough for visitors,' said Alice. Without knowing what she could or couldn't promise, she had to be careful what she offered.

'I hear you've got a young man coming to stay,' said Bernard, pulling himself up straight in the doorway beside his wife.

'Fran's told you already?' said Alice, surprised.

'You didn't mention anything about him in your interview,' said Bernard.

'Should I have?' Alice stared at him defiantly. How dare he?

'This was a post for people without attachments,' said Samantha.

'This was a post like all others advertised under the Equality Act of 2010,' said Alice. 'By which no candidate can be disqualified for anything not pertinent to their ability to do the job.' She was improvising a bit, she didn't know the exact wording or anything – but she didn't care. Her blood was boiling.

'Don't start with all that Equal Opportunities crap,' said Bernard.

Alice stared at him.

'I'm really sorry,' she said, 'but I'm going to have to ask you to put that fire out.'

She turned around and headed straight back down the stairs.


24


After the strangeness and intensity of her first couple of days, the next few passed without incident. Neither the boy nor the woman reappeared and – small, but oh-so-sweet victory – the S-Js did not relight their fire. The

National Committee member whom Fran had mentioned, David Bridge, called her to arrange a couple of cataloguing sessions. He arrived on Monday morning, a tall, softly spoken man, recently retired, who exuded competence. After telling her more about the Committee over coffee, he set about his work swiftly. The report he snail-mailed her a few days later was fantastic, full of detailed information on the condition and estimated age, provenance, and value of over seventy paintings, as well as a few dozen *objets d'art* on which he felt reasonably confident about giving an opinion.

With the memory of her anxiety fading, Alice once again threw herself into a multitude of tasks. On her visit, Fran had suggested that she begin cataloguing some of the books in the library, a relatively easy task which would also help shave consultancy fees. Alice set to this with great pleasure. The unusually laid-out library, essentially a long room with partially sectioned-off areas and cubby holes, was definitely now her favourite place in Bramley. With tall windows on the courtyard-facing wall and plenty of cute, warped diamond-paned ones in the smaller areas, it had a lovely light, and the lower ceiling increased its sense of intimacy. The divided parts included two 'mini' sitting areas with fireplaces, one at either end, a study area, and a larger reading room with three floor-to-ceiling shelves of antique books. Alice imagined the old life of the room, a mother in a sequin dress, her young children playing with a wooden trainset in one sitting area whilst a guest browsed books in another; a man, the *Master of the House,* ruffs bunched at throat and wrists, penning letters in the study.

During her excavation of the cluttered desktop and its drawers in the study she came across one of the older pieces of correspondence between the Trust for England and the S-Js. The letter, which she read with fascination, was from a Richard Long, a Senior Property Developer with the Trust, and it outlined the Heads of Terms agreement for the Trust to take on Bramley. She was amazed at the power it handed to the charity, effectively preventing the S-Js from selling any of the catalogued items and passing ownership of everything to the Trust after their deaths. Whilst they could of course move as they pleased through the house, they were only allowed personal items within their living quarters and could not make any changes, e.g. to decorations, pictures, etc within their rooms without prior agreement in writing from the Trust.

No wonder the poor old S-Js were so narked.

After reading all twelve pages in full, Alice checked the date on it: 10th October 2010. Nine years ago! She marvelled at how long these things could take. Still, she was sure the S-Js would have spent a long time wrangling with this agreement – no matter how impecunious they were.

She took the letter to her office, the converted cloakroom, and placed it in a drawer in her desk. *Her desk that was still pitifully empty, barring her own laptop.* She wondered how long it would be before the tenders came back for the broadband contract. And then how long it would be before the right person in HQ selected one. And then how long before it actually got installed.

Really, this should have all been done before she even started. What had her predecessor done with all her time?

She was beginning to see for herself the truth of the Trust's legendary bureaucracy. Still, at least she had Fran on her side. In her experience, you could cope with a lot

of institutional obfuscation provided your boss was
good.

## 25

After another week she felt she'd had enough of her own
company, interspersed only with the occasional wary
conversation with one of the S-Js, or a smiley encounter
with George. She began to look forward to Matthew's
arrival on the coming Saturday.

It was now well into October and the warm(ish)
weather was starting to wane. She felt it most at night,
her feet growing numb in bed, and wondered when the
first frost would come.

Fran popped in once more with the textile cleaner
she'd requested – promising that the broadband provider
had been selected, and she would get her contract letter
through soon – and Alice spent an afternoon getting
back into Bernard's good books by almost completely
removing the stain on the tapestry. In gratitude, he went
and found her a book in the library on the old Roman
Mystery Religions, which included a section on the
Mithras cult. She read it through eagerly that night,
hooked by the story of a cult that had spread to the far
corners of the Roman Empire and was popular with
soldiers and tradesmen. For a long time its secret
temples, or *Mithrae*, had rivalled Christianity in popularity
amongst the Roman citizens. When Christianity pulled
sharply ahead in the third century BC, largely thanks to a
push from the Emperor Constantine, it sneakily adopted
many of the Mithras myths, including Mithras' birthday
on the 25th December.

The morning after she'd finished the book she was taking it back downstairs to the library when she saw the boy again.

The boy in the burgundy hood.

She was at the half landing, surrounded by giant, colour-leached portraits of Greek gods and heroes, when she felt a quivering in the air. It was close to her left ear, in the shadow of her hair, like the flittering of a moth – or the voice of the ethereal man reading to her when she was a child – and then she felt a whooshing and he came down past her, rushing the final few stairs.

Clutching the leather book, she set off after him, leaping three steps at once, scrambling round the corner past the kitchen and into the vaulted crypt. The red jacket and hood, blurred, misty, carried away quickly by the fleeting spirit within it, dodged left, down a small dark passage and then – she missed it, but it must have happened – he passed straight through the shut door at the end.

Dropping the book by a small statue of a Georgian lady, she ran to the door, fumbled with the key, and shoved it open on to the courtyard.

There was a red flash across the yard, the boy disappearing through the passageway out of Bramley, the bridge across the moat.

Luckily the main gate was open so at least she didn't have to stop again and struggle with a lock. She came out over the stone bridge, checking left and right, catching sight of him scarpering across the lawn in the distance, bright in the full daylight. As his feet flashed up and down she thought one was a different colour to the other, grey, not brown.

Panting, she sped after him.

He reached the long, hydrangea-covered Victorian wall of the Kitchen garden, then found the blue gate and vanished through it – but not before throwing back a brief glance so she had the chance to see his sharp white face, the flushed cheeks – and the rich red of his anorak in the daylight, its quilted, contemporary bulge.

When she came through the gate there was no sign of him in the neat wire-strung beds of the garden. She crossed the brick path through the centre and exited through the opposite gate. Here there was an orchard, leading to the stumpery and woodland.

But no sign of the boy in the burgundy hood.

'Shit,' she muttered.

She walked through the orchard, scanning in between the bare, draping branches of the trees, looking into the mid-distance to see if she could see him.

Nothing.

## 26

As she came back towards the moat she saw someone on the bridge. It was the farmer, Tom Gauge. She slowed, her breath still ragged from chasing the boy, as she approached him.

'Hullo!' he called as she came up. 'You look like you've seen a ghost.'

'Um…' She tugged her hair.

Tom walked up to her, put a hand lightly on her elbow.

'You really do look like you've seen a ghost,' he said.

She shook her head, but she was suddenly confused and nervous and the words weren't coming. Could she tell him?

'Perch here a second,' he said, leading her to the bridge wall. She did as instructed. 'Get your breath back…'

'Did you – did you see somebody – a boy?' she said. 'Back there?'

Tom looked up as she pointed over her shoulder towards the Kitchen garden. 'No,' he said.

'Don't worry,' she said quietly.

He looked at her. 'Who do you think it was? Someone playing truant?'

'I don't know,' she said.

'Shall I take a look?

'No, don't worry.'

'Go on, you go indoors, get a hot drink or something. I'll come back and see you in a minute.'

'No – but come inside. Have a drink with me.'

He studied her face. 'OK,' he said. 'I could do with warming up.'


27


'I was worried about you for a minute back there.'

Alice sipped her coffee. They were sitting at the large pine table in the kitchen.

'Tom, do you know any weird stories associated with this place?' she said.

He looked at her. 'Some,' he said, after a pause.

She felt a huge release of pressure in her chest.

'Like what?' she said.

'I think I've seen something here,' he said. 'A ghost, perhaps.'

More pressure easing. 'Me too,' she said quietly.

'I saw a boy once, too,' he continued. 'Running through the woods. It was – it was broad daylight. As he ran, I saw him going *through* the trees. I had to pinch myself.'

'Wearing a burgundy jacket,' she said.

He nodded.

'Any ideas who it might be?' she said.

'No.'

'Have you spoken to Bernard and Samantha about it?'

'No, I didn't think about it,' he said. 'I saw him when I was in the upper field. But, well – I just didn't want to talk about it after.'

'Strong silent type?' she said, with a small smile.

He nodded. 'Doesn't really fit with the image. I'd pretty much convinced myself it was my imagination.'

'You know, I'm pleased,' she said. 'To know someone else has seen him.'

'At least we're not mad,' he said with a wry grin.

'No. I've seen a woman, too.'

'Where?'

'In my room.'

'Wow, you are attracting them.'

'Yes.'

'You must be frightened, new job, on your own with only a couple of old eccentrics for company plus ghosts…'

She looked up at him. 'I got a bit anxious today when I saw the boy ghost. He was in the house, I followed him out but lost him at the Kitchen garden. But, no – I'm not frightened. Not by ghosts.'

'There's not many people who could say that.'

They both laughed.

'I really love this job,' she said. 'It's what I've always wanted to do. I was thinking of speaking to the others about it – the Smythe-Johnstones, my boss – but then I thought, no, what's the point? It would undermine their opinion of me. They wouldn't believe it.'

'It might not.'

'Really? I think most people would think you're nuts if you told them you'd seen a ghost.'

'Unless they've seen one too.'

'Yes. But –'

'What?'

'I've seen a ghost before.' She wouldn't let on about every incident, in case he thought she really was nuts – at least for now.

'Really, when?'

'When I was a child. He was reading a book to me. But my father, when he came in the room, he couldn't see him. So I think – I think only a few people see them.'

'So best not to tell everyone?'

'Yes.'

'Well, let's you and I form an alliance. Ghost See-ers Anonymous.'

He rolled his eyes a little, then drank some coffee. Alice felt the world returning to normal.

'What are you here for?' she said.

'Just bringing the Smythe-Johnstones their rent,' he said. 'They like their cash now.'

'Hard times,' said Alice, wondering whether he should be paying them or the Trust now.

'As well you know.'

Before they parted at the bottom of the stairs, him on his way up to the S-J's quarters, her on her way to the library, he turned back and said:

'I've enjoyed sharing our experience of the paranormal. Do you fancy lunch on Sunday? Maybe we could go to The Hinde?'

'The Hinde?' she said. Her mouth went dry.

'Yes, the local boozer. Lovely little place, old beams and a fire. Great roasts.'

'Um, I can't. I've got someone coming to stay.'

'Oh, no worries. Another time.'

'Yes. Yes, that would be nice.'


28


The next day, after lunch, she drove to the station to meet Matthew.

She sat for quarter of an hour on the outdoor step of the country station as the arrival time of his train came and went. There were no live bulletins and the ticket desk was closed. At least she had a signal, so was able to check online when the train would arrive. Cancelled. His connection from Telford was cancelled, and the next one wasn't for another fifty minutes. Matthew would probably be texting or calling, but maybe he didn't have a signal, or her phone hadn't received his message yet.

*Technology.*

She stood up, looked around the grey car park with its empty taxi rank and three empty cars. Opposite her, there was a large, plain redbrick building, probably a working man's club, or Conservative Association. It was cold, and she wished there was a café she could sit in.

A seagull passed overhead and settled on the chimney of the redbrick building, miles away from the sea. It looked around for a moment, then spread its giant wings and flew.

She wished she'd brought a book.

She tried to ring Matthew but it went straight to his answerphone. She left a message, asking whether he was on the next train. Then she read the news for a while before stopping to save her data. She would need it for work. She looked at a few recent photos, pictures of her leaving party at Albany Park, Mandy far too drunk, her arm locked around Kelly, the Centre Manager's, neck, far too tight as usual although everyone knew Kelly was married and wasn't interested. Poor Mandy. She scrolled, came to her last photo of her mum, sitting in her red chair, looking in profile out of the netted windows of the nursing home. She looked wistful, wise, *there* in a way she mostly didn't in her last few months. Alice loved that photo. She felt a tear prick her eye.

She slid the phone back into her pocket as a car, a blue BMW, came into the car park and drew up in front of her. A classy-looking woman dropped off a blonde girl, presumably her teenage daughter, who walked past Alice with a smile and disappeared through the barrier on to the platform. The woman drove off, leaving Alice alone again.

She stood and shook herself a bit to warm up. Her phone vibrated in her pocket.

It must be him, she thought, pulling it out. And then she saw the notification.

*Mum.*

Feelings imploded in her, like firework on top of firework in a night-time sky. Hope – the sweetest, briefest hope – followed by grief, anger, hatred, fizzling out into grey, resigned despair. Her hand was shaking as she opened the text.

*hellO swet bwae stampr*

She stared at it for a while, her mind numb.
What was it?
What was her mum trying to tell her?


## 29

'Wow, just look at that place…'

Alice pulled up in front of the house in her old Fiat. Matthew shook his head slowly from side to side. She grinned.

'Unbelievable, huh?'

'You said it. I've seen your pics and everything, but still…'

They got out of the car and crossed the bridge through into the inner courtyard.

'You have got to be kidding me,' said Matthew, looking up and around at the gold clock, the timbered buildings. 'I can't get over this.'

'I think it's going to be one of the…'

'Oop!' Matthew interrupted. 'Someone's spotted us.'

She followed the direction of his gaze to the rooms above the Squire's room.

'Hello, madam,' said Matthew, waving. Samantha S-J vanished from the latticed window she had been watching them from.

'Where did she go?'

'You're probably the first black man in Bramley,' said Alice. 'Something of a treat.'

'Excellent.'

Alice smiled. She felt good, having someone familiar to talk to. Someone funny. It was a breath of fresh air.


## 30

'I can't believe you're doing all this on your own. Hats off, I couldn't.'

It was later in the afternoon and they were lying in the four-poster bed talking and polishing off a bottle of wine that Alice had picked up from Renmore. Matthew had listened as she excitedly recounted all the things – less the paranormal elements – that had happened in her first fortnight, including her interactions with the S-Js, Fran and the mute gardener.

'Why not?' she said.

He looked around at the oak panelling, the detail of the tapestry leached in the fading light of the late afternoon. 'It's just you on your own, isn't it? I like working in a team. Well, a team without Mike,' he added.

She shrugged, running a finger across his lower lip. 'I like it,' she said.

'The responsibility?'

'Yeah. As you say, it's just me. It either succeeds or fails because of me.'

'Don't you get kind of – creeped out. I mean, the old woman, her husband. This *place*?'

She paused. She knew she was going to say something to him this weekend about the ghosts and texts. Just not now.

'No,' she said. 'I love it.'

# 31

The next day they got up early and Alice gave Matthew the tour of the house. She realised that, whilst he did well on appreciation of the layout and atmosphere, his eyes glazed when she went into any detail on the collection. After coffee, she suggested a ride out to explore the area, something she hadn't found time to do yet.

That part of Shropshire was renowned for some shallow sandstone caves called *rock shelters*, which had been worked on by early humans. They visited these first. Matthew had started lessons at a climbing wall back in Farnborough so, egged on by Alice, he tested his skills in the second cave, where there were no tourists. Then they went to Loveton, a long, thin village with a lovely old church, and ate lunch in a lace-curtained tearoom. They tried to hide their amusement from the elderly owner that the 'cake counter' had only one stale Victorian sponge with some biscuits that appeared to have come straight out of a McVities packet and been arranged on small plates. As they left, Alice remembered where she'd heard the village name before; it was the place that George lived.

They were back at Bramley by mid-afternoon. Alice took Matthew off round the grounds. At the lake they stood watching bronze leaves from the splintered limb of the giant beech waltzing down across the water. Alice took hold of Matthew's hand.

'There's something else happening here,' she said.
'What's that?'

'What do you think about ghosts?'

'What – besides the fact they don't exist?'

'I think they do.'

'Why?' he turned and looked at her. 'Are you going to tell me this place is haunted?'

She nodded.

'And you haven't been taking drugs?'

'No.'

'Why do you think so?'

'I've seen one – two ghosts. Here. A boy, running out of the house and vanishing into the gardens. And a woman, with an injury on her hand. Stop smiling!'

'OK, sorry. It's a bit too much for me to take in at once.'

'And – I've had texts from my mum.'

'You what? Your mum? She's dead, isn't she…?'

Alice dug into her jacket pocket and brought out the phone. She showed him the messages.

'See?'

Matthew's expression wavered between a frown and an incredulous smile.

'This can't be from your mum,' he said. 'Someone else has her phone now. The sim card wasn't cleared when it was given, or sold, to the next owner. This is an accidental message. The fact it's gibberish gives it away.'

'That's what I thought at first. But look, it's *hello sweetheart*. She called me sweetheart for the first time ever, in a card, before she died.'

'Maybe she started writing a text she never sent. Then the next owner sent it by accident. Maybe it got passed to one of the other old people in the home, they didn't know one end of the phone from the other…'

'That's not very sensitive,' said Alice.

'Sorry. It's not meant to be insensitive.'

A pair of mallards came down on the water in a splash of green and grey. Alice felt her spirits drop. She wanted to be alone. But Matthew was here until tomorrow afternoon. It suddenly felt like a long time to be with someone she hardly knew.

'Sorry,' he said again.

'It's OK,' she said.

'So – tell me more about these ghosts,' he said.

'Later,' she said. 'Let's walk on a bit, in the wood.'

He looked awkward for a moment, then a little desperate, like he was going to say something else. But all he said was: 'OK.'

## 32

They heard George before they saw him, sawing down hazel wands on a steep, clayey bank amidst the trees. He stopped when they approached.

'George – this is my… friend, Matthew,' said Alice, awkwardly.

George looked up from under his black curls, gave an impish smile.

'Pleased to meet you, George,' said Matthew.

The gardener nodded enthusiastically. Then he pointed at the felled hazel shoots and raised his saw arm to show his muscle.

'Good way to keep fit, mate,' said Matthew.

George touched him lightly on the chest and then shrugged with his hands open.

'Err –' said Matthew.

'He's from Farnborough,' said Alice. 'Like me. We worked together.'

George nodded slowly, like he was measuring it up. Then he pointed at himself, ran quickly through his George and the Dragon routine, then pointed at Matthew, looking the taller man straight in the eye.

'He wants to know your name,' said Alice.

'Oh – Matthew,' said Matthew.

Alice wandered over to the pile of neatly stacked hazel wands. 'Are you laying a hedge…' she began.

'Hey!'

She looked around, just in time to see Matthew shove George's shoulder. The gardener took a step back and glared back defiantly.

'What happened?' she said.

Matthew shook his head, disgusted.

'What happened?' she said again, looking at George.

George shrugged, bewildered.

'Tell me…' she said to Matthew.

'Let's go,' he said, turning abruptly and starting to jog down the muddy bank.

She threw a look at George, who appeared utterly at a loss. 'I'll find out,' she said, then hurried after Matthew, leaving the gardener standing by the wood pile.


33


'What was it?' she said again, as they came past the lake on to the great lawn.

'That guy,' said Matthew.

'What did he do?'

'He did the African grin at me. The *nigga* grin.'

'What?'

'Like this.' Matthew drew back his lips in a rictus grin, showing his teeth. 'While you weren't watching.'

'No, he can't have...'

Matthew gave her a reprimanding glance, still walking.

'He's mute, he was probably doing something else, trying to tell you something...'

'OK. How about I don't believe your ghosts and you don't believe your dumb volunteer's a racist.'

## 34

'Hey...'

Samantha was dragging Henry across the courtyard on his lead as they came through the gates, Alice still struggling to keep up with Matthew's stride.

'Oh, come on you stupid...' the old woman was saying, before she turned and saw them. 'Oh, hello,' she said.

'Hello, Samantha,' said Alice. 'This is Matthew.'

'He's such a pest with bones,' said Samantha, looking back at the stubborn Labrador. She tugged hard on his lead and he made a harsh gagging sound. 'I gave him one in the kitchen. He wants to go back for it. Come on, Henry, we're going for your walk!'

Matthew looked at Alice as the old woman struggled past them with the dog pulling in the opposite direction.

'Pleased to meet you too,' he said quietly, as she disappeared through the sheltered entranceway.

They crossed the quadrangle to the main door.

'She's old,' Alice said.

'Old.'

'I'm not trying to justify her behaviour.'

'Look, I don't care. I expect this kind of thing in the countryside. Sometimes.'

'I believe you,' said Alice. 'About George.'

He nodded.

They went inside.


## 35

They managed to remain friendly over the next twenty-four hours, but by the time Alice dropped Matthew at the station the next afternoon she had to admit, the emotion she felt most was relief.

They kissed on the platform and agreed she would come back to Farnborough next time. She told him she was sorry she hadn't been angry enough on his behalf about George and the brazen rudeness of Samantha and that she would take it up with them.

But, after the train had left and Alice was standing alone on the empty platform, she had to take a deep breath. She had only had one short-lived relationship, and this was the first time she'd spent a long period alone with someone. It was intense, especially with the incidents with George and Samantha. She realised that she was pleased to be back on her own – at least for now. She needed to regroup.

She drove back to Bramley feeling vaguely morose. She felt bad about herself, but also bad about Matthew's lack of empathy for her own story. Did he think she was nuts?

George was sweeping leaves in the drive when she pulled up near the house. She got out of the car and went up to him. He gave her a swift salute.

*Hello boss.*

'George – what did you do to Matthew?' she said.

He boggled his eyes and shook his shoulders.

'He says you made a racist gesture to him. While I wasn't looking.'

George shook his head vehemently.

She looked hard into his dark eyes, then looked down. She put her car keys in her pocket. 'OK,' she said. 'Well you know we practice equal opportunities around here. In accordance with the law. We don't ever – *ever* – discriminate against someone because of their race, colour, gender, sexuality or age.'

He nodded and looked genuinely sheepish, but whether out of guilt or meekness she couldn't tell. Despite what she'd said to Matthew, she really didn't know if he'd done it or not. There was always the possibility he had done some exaggerated expression to try and convey something, perhaps just friendliness. It was his style.

And there was always the possibility he was a racist, subconsciously or not.

'OK,' she said, and turned towards the house.

# A Discovery

## 36

Across November, the weather took a turn for the worse.

The final leaves were whipped from the oaks by a chill wind that blew in across the lake and down over the lawn to shake the windows and groan through the eaves of the house. The rain fell often, heavy and cold. Bramley became a fridge, just about liveable in the late afternoon once the ancient heating system, struggling since dawn, had been helped along by the feeble warmth of the daylight hours. Alice liked hill walking, was used to being outdoors for hours on end in harsh weather, but wondered how she would cope through the winter. First thing she would do with the flood of revenue once the visitors came would be to invest in new central heating. She couldn't take two winters in this temperature.

Fran called and told her of the good news – they had appointed BT to install the broadband – coupled with the bad news, that it wasn't going to happen until after Christmas due to Bramley's remoteness. Alice informed her that things were getting seriously difficult for her now without access to the internet. She had made copious notes on her laptop, but she needed access to a heap of documents on the Trust's system – policies, procedures, guidance and best practice on new property, etc. She had done as much 'informal' research, planning and cataloguing as she could. She had made copious notes but needed to start proper business and operations planning, and to flesh out her marketing and communications strategy (preferably with major input from the Trust Comms team). She needed to start prioritising real tasks and employing contractors and recruiting volunteers to support her in painting and repairing and tidying up the house. Bramley needn't be perfect for the quiet, informal opening she planned – but it needed to be a lot better than its current state.

Fran heard all she was saying and told her she would do all she could to help things along. In the interim she sent a paper copy of Bramley's Development Plan, which Alice read in earnest and found deeply disappointing. At twelve pages and containing unimaginative actions like 'Install Security System' and 'Catalogue collection', she wondered how much they had paid the consultant to do it. No matter what, they had been robbed. Even she could have done better.

She was clearly on her own with this one. Still, at least when she took a trip into the nearby town for groceries and checked her bank account she found she had finally been paid. For the first month, if not for the second. Good job she still had cash left in the bank, after all her mum's care and accommodation bills.

## 37

'You look like you could do with some help?'

Alice looked up from where she was, down on her hands and knees in the mud, prodding a long stick into the lake. Tom Gauge was standing above her. She smiled.

'I didn't hear you coming,' she said, then added: 'I think the feeder pipe to the moat is blocked. I've been trying to find George but he's not around.'

Tom followed her gesture and saw the water brimming around the bank closest to the house. The mud there was becoming waterlogged. He knelt down beside her and rolled up his sleeve.

'I wonder how old this feeder pipe is,' he said. 'Here, let me…'

'No, it's freezing, you don't want…' began Alice, but the farmer had already plunged his arm into the lake. He twisted to look up at the slate sky, giving himself extra reach and balance as he felt around.

'You're right,' he said, rummaging. 'It's bloody freezing. Bloody, bloody freezing.'

'Can you feel anything?'

'Yes, it's a piece of wood, I think. Just caught… on… something. Ah! Come on, you bastard!'

Suddenly he pushed himself up, bringing his arm out of the water. The thing he brought out was dark and covered in weed, as thick as Alice's wrist, but as soon as she saw it she realised it wasn't a stick. It was a shoe, a pump, the canvas top stained greeny-brown, the sole beige.

'Look at that,' said Tom, scooping some black sticks and weed out of the pump. 'There were a few rocks lodged around it, and something unpleasantly slimy…'

'Wonder how that got there,' said Alice, looking at his mud-streaked hand. 'But thank you! I don't think my stick would have done the job.'

'Probably not,' he said.

'Your sleeve is sopping. You need to wash.'

'Yes.'

'Come inside and warm up. You here for the usual – to pay the rent?'

'Yes. And yes, OK, I will.'

'I've got some homemade soup if you want some. I was going to have it once I'd sorted this.'

'Sounds good.'

'Lentil and courgette?'

'Hmm. Lovely.'

She smiled at the face he pulled. And wondered again how a pump had got to the bottom of the lake.

38

They went into the kitchen. At some stage the room had been refitted with seventies duck-egg blue Formica units, meaning it could hardly be described as homely – but at least it was warm. Tom popped the shoe in the bin and then washed his hands in the sink.

'I'm spending half my time in here these days,' said Alice. 'It's the only place that's not an absolute ice bucket.'

'What would we country folk do without our Agas?' said Tom.

'Here – if you sit against this bit, you can dry your sleeve while you eat.'

Tom obediently pushed one of the wooden chairs beside the old cooker and pressed his wet arm against it.

'Smashing,' he said.

Alice smiled. 'Haven't heard someone say that since uni,' she said.

'Ah'reet cocker, I'll have a bacon and egg barm for me lunch, please.'

'It's freezing, put wood in th'owl!'

They chuckled. Alice retrieved the Tupperware container in the fridge with her soup and tipped it into a saucepan.

'How you settling in?' he asked, as she placed the pan on the Aga and spun the green liquid with a wooden spoon.

'Fine,' she said. 'The Trust is proving a bit slow in getting me some of the things I need.'

'Like what?'

'Broadband, for one.' She realised she should be careful. There was a line to be held with your employer.

'And the lovely owners?'

'No problems.'

'Last time I saw her, Samantha said you'd had a friend visit.'

Alice was surprised. 'Oh she did, did she?'

'Sorry – none of my business.'

Alice paused. 'No, don't worry. I had someone from my old work come to stay for the weekend. What did she say?'

'Well, nothing more than that, really.'

She decided to change the subject. 'Have you seen any more ghosts lately?'

He shook his head. 'No. Not again. You?'

'No. Nothing for a month now. If you hadn't corroborated my story I might think I was going nuts.'

'Stuck out in the country with nothing to do.'

'All work and no play makes Alice a dull girl.'

'Not that bad I hope.'

'No, I'm not going to be picking up an axe anytime soon.'

'Well, let me know if you fancy going out for a drink sometime. To relieve the monotony.'

Alice smiled. 'Yes – that would be nice.'


## 39

Despite the dismal weather, Alice went about her chores with a new brightness that afternoon.

She went back to the lake – waving to George, now reappeared from nowhere and removing dead annuals from the far-side border of the lawn – and checked that the pipe was still working properly. Then, with a clutch of stakes from the Kitchen garden, she marked out the route of her proposed path to the upper field vantage point. Finally, she came back to the house and tried to match the wall colours in the small dining room and Squire's room with a heritage paint catalogue she had ordered. She thought she had made the perfect finds, smiling at the marketing of the names the company had given their paints – *Puck*, *Hidey Hole*, and *Goblin*. Straight out of a fantasy novel, which was kind of what you wanted, in a tacky sort of way. The recreation of Olde England, an enchanted place of church bells, village greens and the crack of leather on willow, as opposed to the gruelling twelve-hour shifts in factories and fields.

She used a tape measure and calculator to work out how many litres she would need, recording it all on her laptop. Soon, policy or no policy, she was going to have to start recruiting volunteers to help with clearance, with the cleaning and painting. She knew how to manage volunteers from her old job, so what if she didn't follow the Trust's policies to the T?

As usual, by the time she'd finished her tea – this time, just baked beans on toast – she was exhausted. But she knew that she had to do one thing.

She must call Matthew.

She checked her phone and found a pleasing three bars of reception. Now was the moment. And yet why did she feel so... anxious?

She dialled the number.

It rang for a while and she was beginning to feel a slightly guilty sense of relief, she could leave a message, put it off for a while – and then he answered.

'Hi hun,' he said.

'Hi.'

'How's things in the woods?'

'Pretty good,' she said. She told him a little about her recent tasks, as well as how cold it was in bed.

'Need a man to warm you up,' he said.

'Too right,' she said, laughing. 'How's Albany Park doing?'

'Kelly's bid to the Lottery didn't come off.'

'Did they give any feedback?'

'Actually, yeah, some useful stuff. They didn't mind the overhead costs but they felt the project costs should be beefed up some, to make it proportionate to the scale of what we wanted to do.'

'So they want you to resubmit?'

'Yes.'

'Good news.' She knew how important getting the Lottery funding through would be to the centre. Without it, she wouldn't be surprised if they were closing – or at least in line for some serious redundancies – in a couple of years' time.

'So – when are you coming down to see me?' he asked.

'Well, I've been thinking. How about in between Christmas and the New Year?'

'That's ages…'

'Only a month.'

'And a half. And it's already been a fortnight since we saw each other.'

'But there's a lot I have to do here. We're opening in April and we haven't even started preparing the building.'

'Hm.' There was a moment's pause and then Matthew said: 'Did you take it up with your employers, the racism?'

She hadn't been expecting that. She paused for a moment and then said: 'I spoke to George.'

'And Samantha? Did you report it to your boss?'

'George said he hadn't meant it, what you saw…'

'You didn't take it up?'

'I didn't see it, it's just – it's one person's word against another's…'

'So you *didn't* believe me?'

'I did – but…'

'There is no buts. You should have supported me.'

'We would have to go through a whole process, it would be really difficult for me living here with them on my own every night and day. Samantha didn't actually say anything, and with George, because I didn't see it, we wouldn't be able to prove anything if he continued to deny it. Which of course he would.'

'It puts down a marker. So when you have your visit from the Telford Goan Society or whoever and they report something similar, you start to build a case. To stop it happening again.'

'I spoke to George. Very clearly.'

'But you need to take it up with Fran too.'

This time Alice paused.

'Well, will you?'

'If anything else happens remotely…'

'You aren't going to, are you?'

'I'll think about it…'

'No. It's not happening. Which means – which means we're not happening, either.'

'What?'

'Sorry.'

'You mean…?'

'Yes. I need someone more committed to me than that.'


## 40

She was crying when the call ended.

Her finger hovered over the redial button for ages before she saw the reception suddenly vanish. She chucked the phone down on the bed.

How could it have gone so wrong, so suddenly?

He was right of course, she should have reported it. And she would, she decided, she would let Fran know. But still something felt wrong, unbalanced in their relationship. He had been so dismissive of her, when she told him about the ghosts. Which, even though hard – very hard – to believe, she knew was true.

She hadn't been expecting such a swift change in her life. She wondered if this was it, or whether they would speak to each other again, make up. Depressed, she tried reading for a while, but struggled to concentrate.

Finally, she mustered the energy to go and brush her teeth in the sink in the garderobe, then crawled into her chilly bed.

Within moments, she was asleep.

## 41

There was something damp, oily, brushing against her forehead, tickling her fringe.

She realised it was *her*, the anxious woman. It was her hand. The greasy sensation was her wound. The cut was leaking something, a little pus, on to her face, on her hair. She groaned.

And, with a severe breath, opened her eyes. Wide.

The afterimage of the ghost, leaning over her, stroking her face, was in her mind.

Was she there, in the dark?

She wasn't there. The room was quiet. Empty.

Alice's heart tugged against her ribs, like a wild animal in a cage.

She wasn't afraid of ghosts, remember?

Was this another visitation, after so long quiet?

She sat up in bed, grasped and shook her phone to light the torch.

The woman was there, at the window beside her, her mouth open, showing her large white front teeth. Buck teeth.

'OK,' said Alice. 'I know you want something. Tell me – show me what you want.'

Once again, the woman looked down through the window towards the woods, the lake. But instead of plunging through it and vanishing, she turned and ran straight out through the bedroom door – which of course remained closed.

'Shit,' said Alice.

She was going to have to act fast. She sprang from her bed and threw on her fleece, shoved her feet into her slippers and flung open the door.

'God!'

The woman was right in front of her, staring into her face. The beam of Alice's phone was directed straight into her stomach. At the edge of the torchlight, the woman's eyes were wide, her nostrils flared. She looked antagonistic, shy, churlish all at once. Revolted.

Alice took a step back. The woman scowled.

Something in Alice's mind, a deep, half-buried memory, shifted and she remembered the man, sitting on his lap as a child, how he had made her feel safe. Her dad had come in the room – but nothing had changed in her position, she hadn't fallen back on to the settee – she had been sitting *in* the man. She was sure of it.

Taking a deep breath, Alice stepped forward and leaned into the woman.

## 42

*She was running, almost breathless, up the grand old staircase. Glancing up past the leaded windows she saw the giant paintings, old men with curly beards and naked, milk-white women, mucking about in woods and ponds, a guy with goat's feet.*

*Behind her the sound of footsteps – boots – pounding on floorboards. She shrieked and sprang up the steps two at a time, pumped up on adrenaline and much, much more.*

*'I'm coming to find you…'*

*She panicked, like it was real, as she reached the landing, glanced both ways, then darted off left towards the bedroom. Through the windows on her right she saw the courtyard below, the covered walkway that led to the gate and bridge across the moat. There was a dark flash on the cobbled stones, a monster, a wolf, no – crazy girl! – a dog, you're seeing things, it's just that slobbery pup.*

*She heard a thumping sound and glanced over her shoulder. He was at the top of the stairs in his ridiculous floppy hat, grinning like a madman, turning and chasing after her.*

*She screeched again, reached the panelled door and shoved it open. Beyond was the bedroom, their bedroom. She dived in, slammed the door behind her and sprinted over to the second, smaller door. She opened it and shut herself in the bare closet with its sink and tiny, open window, warm with afternoon sunlight. She grabbed the latch and tried to stop her ragged breathing, her hammering heart.*

*She waited, thinking, wondering, how could all this ever happen to her? She rested her forehead on the door, sniffing the almost vinegary scent of the old wood.*

*She heard the bedroom door open. Once again he called, 'I'm coming!'*

*She smiled, couldn't control a sudden snort.*

*'I can hear you...'*

*She heard his footsteps thumping across the room. She lifted the sleeve of her dress to try and muffle another snort, noticed a little blood on it as she pulled it back. Yuck, a bloody nose – too much coke.*

*She giggled, her head a sudden riot of colours, red, blue, yellow, black. The latch clicked up, despite her feeble attempt to hold it. She drew back against the wall as the door began to open.*

*'Joker...' she shouted, laughing, at the same time feeling a little nauseous.*

*Then, from outside, from somewhere down the garden, there was a loud crack, followed by a splash.*

*She turned quickly to the window.*

43

And then Alice was back to herself, alone in the dark corridor, the woman gone.

She breathed in deeply and stepped across the landing. Had she just shared the memory of a ghost? She grabbed the handrail that ran beneath the mullioned windows and gazed at the courtyard below. In the faint moonlight she could just make out the hunched laurels, the gold clock, the box planters in the middle of the cobbling.

And the boy. The boy in the hood, standing by the planters, staring up at her.

'Sheesh,' she said. 'Are you two working together now?'

She looked down at him. He stood his ground. In the poor light she sensed as much as noticed how gaunt he was, how his features were sharp, feral, under-fed.

'OK,' she said, 'I'm coming.'

She didn't know whether she was seeing things or going mad but – yes, there was no doubt about it, this felt like an adventure.

She ran down the landing, down the stairs, and out through the door into the courtyard in her pyjamas, fleece and slippers. The boy turned and fled for the gate as soon as she appeared. She ran after him, scarcely noticing the cold.

There was no noise, no scuffing of trainers against stone – as usual – so she had to guess where he was going, to follow him out over the bridge, across the soft grey of the forecourt, up the path and through the Kitchen garden gate.

The Kitchen garden was simple to navigate in the moonlight, following the brick paths in between the neat, cleared rectangles of the vegetable beds. She reached the opposite gate and moved into the orchard, far creepier with its sculptured, densely branched trees like dark anemones. She saw a shape, boy-sized, at the other end of the area, near the start of the woods and the stumpery. As soon as she saw him, his shuffling – he was gone.

Alice stopped for a moment, catching her breath. She felt her courage falter, as if a single icy drop of fear had struck the calm pool of her senses and sent out a ripple of doubt.

What was she going to do?

Slowly, she began to move forward. Clearly, the ghosts of Bramley had wanted her to come this way. They had wanted her to go… to the stumpery.

As she stepped forward she half saw and half felt the fruit trees around her. She had an uncanny sensation that they were alive – which of course they were, albeit dormant – and... and that they were watching her. Shifting slightly to follow her movement, even though the night was perfectly still.

She needed to keep a lid on her overactive imagination.

Towards the end of the orchard the route became even darker, with a thicker bank of scrub and trees rising up before her. She couldn't see it, but knew the stumpery was not far away, maybe thirty foot, hidden in the blackness of those trees. There was no sign of the boy.

And then she heard it.

A faint, ever-so-faint, high-pitched sound.

Whistling.

Her heart, temporarily settled as she had made her way through the orchard, sprang into action again. She felt the skin shrink on her forehead, around her ears. Her eyes widened.

Someone was whistling up ahead.

In the darkness. Softly, as if under their breath.

And then there was a loud *chink*, metal against stone.

Who was there?

Alice knew she couldn't go on. She could feel her legs shaking. She feared they wouldn't get her back to the house.

She turned and found that actually they were fine, they worked perfectly, and they got her back inside the courtyard of the medieval manor almost before she knew it.

## 44

If her room hadn't been fitted with a Yale lock she was sure she would have woken up the S-Js as soon as she got back. But it was and so, even though the lock wouldn't keep out the ghosts, she decided to try and get some desperately needed sleep. She could think all this through in the morning.

Nevertheless, it took a long time for her mind to let go of its insistent thoughts. Her skull felt like a barrel, rolling around and around over the same few questions. Who were the ghosts? What did they want her to do? Who was it chasing the woman around the house? What was that loud crack she'd heard out of the window?

And what was that whistling – which sounded so very human?

She thought she would never get to sleep and then…

## 45

She woke.

The room had a muted light, the curtains as always only partly drawn.

It was morning.

She checked her phone: 7:48. At least she'd managed a few hours' dreamless slumber. She climbed out of bed and dressed, then headed downstairs. Before breakfast, she knew she had to go back and check the place where the woman and boy had been leading her.

The stumpery.

The morning was cold, the light soft and grey. It was the kind of morning she expected to see fog but, aside from a slight haze on the pond, there was none. Soon she was at the stumpery, examining its peculiar arrangement of short-cut, upended trunks.

She knew nothing about stumperies. The only thing she'd heard was an anecdote about Prince Charles who, when he'd shown his father his, was asked by the Duke when he planned to burn it. Peering at the exposed, jutting roots, Alice wondered about this strange Victorian feature. Whilst there was something fascinating about seeing the knotty part of the tree that normally never saw daylight, she didn't particularly *like* it. It was too awkward, artificial. The best that could be said for it was that it was a good place for growing ferns and shade lovers. Someone had put some hostas in between two fallen yews, but they had been ravaged by slugs.

She stepped off the path and made her way between the trunks, taking care not to crush plants. It wasn't a huge area, about twenty foot by ten, dug into a bank which rose steeply to a denser, more natural mix of scrub and trees.

She weaved in between a sawn trio of trunk rounds, set apart as stools – and then stopped.

Beyond the large, striated trunk of a sweet chestnut up to the left, she spotted something unusual – a gap in the ground between the bronze-green fern fronds. She moved forward and peered over the stump to take a closer look.

She saw that a sizeable trench, longer than a man, had been dug into the soil. It was perhaps three feet wide at the top, but slanted down towards the centre, meaning the gap at the bottom – and it was a gap, a real, long, black gap – was perhaps only a few inches wide.

'What on earth is that...?' she muttered.

She stepped over the trunk and crouched beside the trench. She peered into the long dark slit.

Nothing. Nothing but blackness.

She reached for her phone, shook the torch on, and pointed it into the hole.

Still nothing.

How deep was it? She looked around until she found a stone, which she released over the centre of the hole.

She thought – although she couldn't be sure – that she heard a small scuff, as if it had hit dry ground. Quickly, she looked around for another.

This time, she got down on her hands and knees and leaned out over the hole before she dropped the pebble, tipping her head to listen.

Hmm… She was sure she heard it hit the ground.

She stood up, wondering.

It was obvious who had dug the hole. George had dug it. She had seen him doing it on her first morning.

But why? What was he trying to reach?

Then she thought about her experience the night before. The soft whistling – and the other sound, the chinking sound. Could that have been the sound of a spade, striking the ground?

And if so… what about the whistling? Could mute people whistle?

She felt a sudden sensation, a change in the atmosphere, a renewed eeriness. Everything became more vivid and yet somehow less real, the gloom of the canopy, the jagged stumps like horned stegosauruses scattered around her. The roots seemed urgent, aghast, an insult to the natural order. They shouldn't be here, displayed like this. She recognised this sensation, an acute, painful self-awareness, the foregrounding of her perception, her mind, in her relationship with the world.

It was the first step towards panic.

No.

She sat down on a stump. She wasn't going to let it happen again.

Focus. She focused on the detail of her thought.

Had George been out in the middle of the night, digging and whistling? She couldn't see it. Excepting the blip with Matthew – if that were true – she had warmed to the volunteer gardener, his surprising and gentle humour. Whilst she needed Google on this one, she didn't think mute people could whistle. And why on earth would he be out at night, when he could do the same job during the day?

But if it wasn't George, who was it?

The boy in the hood? Or maybe another ghost? But she had heard a sound, and the ghosts – so far – did not make sounds. Nor did they interact with physical objects.

It was a mystery she realised she wouldn't solve now. Not when the feelers of anxiety were beginning to reach into her brain. No, she needed to get back to familiar surroundings. To get some food inside her.

Then she would think what to do.

46

*hellO swet bwae stampr*

Sitting at the kitchen table, drinking tea, Alice stared at her mum's text.

Hello sweetheart. Beware stumpery.

109

Was that what she meant? Was her mum trying to tell her not to go to the stumpery from across the grave?

Alice gazed at the letters on her phone but what she saw was her mum, not prematurely frail with dementia but skipping about on a half-bright, half-shadowed beach, swishing her dolphin scarf across the back of her neck as she danced and sang one of the latest pop songs. Alice had almost forgotten how carefree, how zany, her mum could be. Later that day, on the seafront promenade, she had blobbed her cheeks and the tip of her nose with her ice-cream to make Alice laugh.

She came back into the room, the here and now. She had to speak to George about why he was digging up there. What was the cavity below the stumpery? How did he know it was there?

Yes, she needed to speak to George. But she needed someone else to confide in. The obvious *someone* was Tom. But she didn't have his number and wasn't sure she could find his house. She wasn't even sure how she'd feel, turning up on his doorstep. Would he think she was a stalker, a bunny boiler like Glenn Close in *Fatal Attraction*?

She guessed he would understand, given that he'd also seen the boy in the hood. But still, maybe she should wait for him to turn up at Bramley again?

But that might not be until next month, when he came to pay his rent…

She turned and looked out of the window. She was too high up to see the moat, but she could see the great lawn and in the distance the tree-lined bank that partly shielded the feeder lake. A pair of thrushes were bouncing about near the bird table in the centre of the lawn. Despite its greyness, the sky had an odd brightness about it, a steeliness. It looked especially cold and she wondered whether snow might be on its way.

The next moment George appeared, plodding along the moat side path with a wheelbarrow brimful of gravel. Alice jumped up and banged on the window. He seemed to tilt his head towards the building, but then carried on pushing the wheelbarrow.

'Silly cow, he's deaf,' Alice muttered to herself. She rushed through to the library, snatched up a pad and pen from the study area where she had been working yesterday, then went out through the quadrangle to the bridge, where she intercepted him. She gestured wildly and he waved, set the barrow down and came towards her.

'Come into the house,' she said. She could feel the air temperature had fallen, even in the last hour. A freeze was definitely on the cards.

When they reached the kitchen door, George stopped and pointed at his muddy boots.

'Kick 'em off,' she said.

He did so, revealing green woollen socks with a darned hole in the left one. He followed her through into the warm kitchen.

'Tea, coffee?'

He made a T with his hands. She flicked the kettle on.

'It's getting very cold,' she said.

He nodded and grabbed the sides of his arms.

'Might snow.'

He raised his eyebrows in agreement.

'George, there's something I wanted to ask you. I've got a pen and pad.'

He picked up the pen and held it above the paper, watching her.

'Can you tell me about that trench you're digging, over in the stumpery?'

He tipped his head and began writing. Alice moved closer to decipher his small, scratchy script.

There's a cave under there, he wrote.

'Really?' she said.

Yes, there's caves round here. U know rock shelters nr Oreton?

'Yes. I went there.'

I was digging dead fern & found a rock. Moved it & saw gap under. Been digging it out 2 c what's there.

'I see,' said Alice. 'Sounds like you need to be careful. The ground could collapse.'

He looked at her, his dark eyes shining. Then he wrote: Yes.

'Yes,' she repeated. 'You're digging it in a very… orderly way.'

Again he looked at her intensely.

Felt safer like that, he wrote. Was worried 2 about ground.

That made sense, she thought. It was a more stable way to investigate it.

'You're not doing any more now, are you?' she said. 'We mustn't take any risks. I can get the Trust to check it out.'

Cd b good hook 4 visitors? he wrote. Come c Bramley caves!

'Yes. The sandstone caves of Bramley…' Alice laughed and looked at him.

She still wasn't completely convinced. She wanted to ask him if he could whistle. Instead, she said:

'Where are you gravelling?'

Filling holes on drive, he wrote.

'Good man. The suspension on my car won't cope much longer.'

He pointed at his eye and then the window.

'You saw,' she said.

He nodded and took a final slug of his tea.

Anything else? he scribbled.

'No, that's all,' she said. 'Just promise me you won't go digging anymore holes until we've checked the ground is safe.'

He put his hand on his heart and mouthed *I promise*.

Then he stood up.

'Thanks then, Jerry,' she said.

Immediately he stopped and gave her a comical frown.

'What?' she said.

He leaned back on the table and drew a small, surprisingly accurate outline of the mouse from the cartoon. Then he put a question mark beside it and stared at her, his mouth open in a smile.

'Tom and Jerry?' she said.

U called me Jerry! he wrote.

'Oh my God, I didn't,' she said. 'I'm so sorry! Fran was talking to me about the other gardener who was called Jerry. I'm really sorry, just a slip of the tongue. Please forgive me.'

He raised his palm to her. No problem.

Then he turned and was gone.

She still wasn't convinced. There was something going on with him.

## 47

When things became especially intense in the house, it helped her to get in the car and take the twenty-minute drive to town. The presence of dozens of ordinary folk pottering up and down between shops, intent on their purchases, was a great leveller. This – in some ways – was also what life was all about. Not medieval ideals, ghosts, grand gardens and art, just the day-to-day requirement of putting food on the table, keeping your home comfortable. She stood underneath the looped aquamarine letters of the Co-op and for a moment felt she could weep with relief.

She traipsed around the bright, neon-lit aisles of the supermarket, stacking up on her usual supply of tins, cereals, frozen meals, a few fresh veggies, milk and bread. She had never been a particularly keen cook and the punishing regime she was under – or more accurately, that she was keeping herself under – meant she had little surplus energy to spend time in the kitchen. She shopped for whatever shortcuts she could find, living out days on Weetabix, baked beans and pizza.

When she emerged from the shop the tiniest dots of white were meandering down from the sky. A memory of her Australian cousin breaking one of her little loved toys came back to her, how she had made herself cry to gain sympathy and attention. It felt like the sky was forcing itself to snow.

Saddled up with cloth bags full of heavy tins, she waddled through the car park at the rear of the store towards her car. She filled her boot, then climbed into the driver's seat. She turned the key, listening as the ignition turned over – then ground to quiet. She clicked the key around again and breathed a sigh of relief as the engine caught. She'd always had trouble with the electrics and particularly the battery, despite having it both recharged and replaced by a range of mechanics. She hoped it wasn't going to go into another one of its bad phases, especially with the remoteness of Bramley and the cold weather coming. It was going to be months before she could afford a new one.

Especially if the Trust carried on with their track record of not paying her.

She drove down the exit road from the car park, in between the store and a high brick wall, and paused at the main road, waiting for an opening in the bundle of cars that had decided to make the sleepy high street busy all of a sudden.

She peered into the cars as they passed, noticing an old Asian couple in a Mercedes, a young girl with her hair stretched back from her face in a ponytail that looked like masochism, a blue Land Rover with – Tom!

And with someone – a man – beside him in the passenger seat. Alice twisted her neck as the car drove past. The large shoulders, green coat, short, thick hair – no, it wasn't a man, it was Fran, wasn't it? It really looked like Fran.

Two more cars passed in front of her. What could Fran be doing here, in a car with Tom?

She was curious enough to turn and follow them, despite it not being the right way back. But straight away she was slowed by the cars in front of her. She saw the Land Rover take a turn off down a side street. Then she came to a red light and had to wait for a family with a young mum and middle-aged dad, the father shouting at his unruly toddler who wanted to do anything in the road except cross it.

By the time the lights turned green Alice realised there was no point in following. She drove past the road they'd gone down, one with a few shops that she thought ultimately continued out of town.

She wondered what they could be doing together. Was it Fran? It had looked a bit like her, but it might have been a man. If it was her, perhaps she had been over to visit Alice at Bramley – although she hadn't let her know she was coming.

Alice shrugged. It probably wasn't Fran. She would ask her next time she saw her.

Just in case.

## 48

By the time she was back at Bramley she had convinced herself it wasn't her manager in the car with Tom. It was more likely to be a labourer – or anyone else from Tom's life, what did she know about him anyway?

But Fran was on her mind now and she was becoming increasingly irritated, verging on cross. Her anger had been growing slowly over the last couple of weeks. At first she'd tried to deny it, to keep it away, for fear of tainting what she still knew to be the best opportunity she'd ever had. Ever. But she could no longer keep it back. The Trust for England – embodied through its Regional Manager – was not doing a good job of getting Bramley ready to be brought to life for the public. Not so far.

She was meant to be opening in just over four months' time and she didn't have a proper Development Plan, David Bridge had been helpful but she needed more support with the catalogue, and she didn't have any volunteers or a budget to spend. She didn't have broadband! How could she carry on like this? She loved Bramley and could easily fill her days pottering about like now – but not happily, not when she knew there were so many things that needed doing.

Things she couldn't do without the Trust doing what *they* were supposed to do. They needed to fulfil their part of the bargain. She began to wonder just how much they cared about Bramley. Was this the real reason her predecessor had left? She'd begun to wonder if it was the ghosts, but perhaps she just got fed up with the incompetence of the organisation. Maybe the Trust for England had bigger fish to fry at the moment?

When she turned off the engine she dug her phone out of her pocket and checked the signal. She growled when she saw the single bar. No hope in ringing Fran straight away. But she needed to set up a meeting, and urgently. She fired off a quick text requesting one as soon as possible.

Then she carried her shopping into the kitchen and made herself some cheese on toast. Outside, it was still snowing in the feeblest kind of way, so after she had finished she went into the library. She pulled an armchair over to the window and sat almost on top of the lukewarm iron grates of the radiator, flicking through some of the actions in one of her many notepads.

She sat there for a quarter of an hour, struggling to concentrate.

It was no good. The frustration with her lack of organisational support, coupled with the little matter of two ghosts, two texts from her dead mother, and a gardener she wasn't sure she could trust, were playing havoc with her mind.

What was she going to do?

She thought guiltily about Matthew. It felt so long since their conversation. And she still hadn't brought the incident up with Fran. She hadn't had a chance to. And now… she knew that that was it, he'd meant what he said. They were over.

Her melancholy was lifted by a faint, thumping vibration that she knew to be one of the S-Js coming down the stairs. She looked out across the courtyard with its salt-sized snowflakes and saw the main door beside the Great Hall open. Bernard emerged in a knee-length waterproof jacket and gumboots, with Henry at his side. She wondered if the dog were arthritic, the way it trudged with an asymmetric step alongside its owner, towards the covered exit.

Bernard didn't turn and see her. Given the state of the windows, the years of unwashed dust and grime, she didn't think he'd spot her even if he did. Soon he was gone with the dog, disappeared past the laurel trees.

Alice turned back, looked at her notes, then gazed towards the fireplace. Her eyes lifted to the grand painting of the bull above the mantelpiece.

It was a magnificent portrait, with all that packed muscle and those calm eyes, measured, unshakeable. She wondered whether there were any more muscular creatures living on the earth. Tigers? Hippos? Lions?

Lions and bulls…

Italy.

She remembered the conversation she'd had way back on her first day with Samantha, sitting in front of that painting. When she'd tried to plug her for stories about Bramley, Samantha had instead just talked about a great-grandfather who brought back that picture and other artefacts from Italy. What had she called him? It was an unusual name. Like the name of a bank or something. But not Barclay. Nor Lloyd. Nor Natwest for that matter, she thought, giggling for the first time since Matthew had been up.

Why had Samantha gone on that trajectory? Alice thought about her early sweep of the building, noticing those art pieces that had been neglected, and those which had been placed in prime or protected positions. She had thought then that the ones which seemed most valued were probably the ones Forbes – *Forbes, that was it!* – had brought back.

So what?

Perhaps she should look a little more into this Forbes chap. She got up and walked to the bookshelves in the study area. She looked along the leather spines, brown with a few blues, framed and lettered in gold and silver. *Practical Knowledge for All, vols I-VI, The Oxford Book of English Verse 1915, Genesee Fever* by Carl Carmer, *Man's Great Adventure* by Parlow…

There.

She tipped her ear towards her shoulder as she looked down at a small, blue drawer with a bronze handle. Crazy – she had felt the sweet, fuzzy vibration of someone speaking in her ear. A man, a man's low voice, soft, almost a whisper. She looked behind her.

There was, of course, no one there. She remembered the moment on the sofa, when she was a small girl, sitting on someone's knee, looking at the book with pictures. The man speaking in her ear. The man who wasn't there.

It was the same voice. Although, as soon as she thought that, she realised she would never know it for certain. How would she know?

But the connection across time, across two immeasurable decades of life and experience, was made. It might be her imagination, but it was there. Her ghost had spoken, her guardian angel.

She lifted the little age-blackened handle and pulled open the drawer.

Inside there were two books, one black, the other brown, a thick-nibbed, red-and-gold Parker fountain pen without its lid, and a few papers. Carefully, she lifted the black book. Its spine was loose, just kept in place by a few stringy cords of the binding. There was no text on the front. She opened the cover and saw that it was a journal, written in ink.

The front page, stained with the watery browns of old ink and age, had only two words, written in capitals: OSTIA ANTICA. She turned the page and read in an obsessively tight, orderly script:

*11ᵗʰ June 1867*

*I reached Ostia by charting a riverboat down the Tiber. The village, once the port of Rome, now lies two miles inland amidst marshes that sweat and stink in the heat. Ostia is a sweet medieval Village with a quaint Castle but for me there was nothing of interest there. I was come solely for the nearby Excavation, ordered by "His Holiness Pius IX".*

*I wished to see for myself the Amphitheatre, the Capitolium, above all the Ancient Temples. For months nearly two hundred*

*Prisoners, under the guidance of Italian Archaeologists Ercole and Visconti, had been sleeping in the Rocco, digging out the Monuments by Day, sweating under the Sun, ravaged to Death by a million Midges.*

*Above all, I was there to see the Mithrae, at least half a dozen of them, with possibly more to discover.*

Alice flicked ahead a few pages, found more details on the traveller's trip to Ostia – or rather to Ostia Antica, as the excavation site was known. She turned to the back, found a few cuttings from an Italian newspaper with illustrations of the site, including one of a visit by the Pope, Pius IX. The Pope, dressed in a long, folded hat, was reaching forward to consider a broken piece of decorated plinth. He was guided by an enthusiastic gentleman.

There was no reference as to who had written the journal but Alice was pretty sure it must have been Forbes. She checked the second book. Again, it was a handwritten journal, but this did contain Forbes' full name in the front – Forbes William James Johnstone. However, it was written in a very different style. Her eyes skimmed phrases: *The Cosmic Order itself rests on the Tauroctony … allowing the Sun and Moon to come into Being… Initiation from Corax, or Raven, to Nymphus, the Bridegroom…*

The writing was more impassioned than the other journal, almost feverish in places. Forbes was clearly taken by his subject matter, which appeared to be some kind of cult. She wondered whether he had written it before or after visiting Ostia Antica.

She picked up the sheets beneath the books. They included more clippings from newspapers, both Italian and English, mainly on the progress of various archaeological digs. Alice knew that the Victorian era saw a great blossoming of interest in ancient sites, the start of a renewed flourishing of archaeology, anthropology and classical study.

And then, as she carefully turned the crisp sheets, she came across something completely out of place, that made her freeze.

It was a photograph.

A photograph of the ghost woman.

49

'Found something interesting?'

Alice spun round to see Samantha in the doorway of the library. She clutched the photo as the old woman walked towards her.

'No, nothing special,' said Alice. She began to replace the photo amidst the papers, then realised she was acting too quickly, suspiciously.

'I found this photo amongst these old papers,' she said. She held the picture up to Samantha who stooped to look at it. The old woman lifted a pair of reading glasses that hung around her neck and put them on. She was wearing a grey-and-brown tweed jacket and Alice noticed the fraying at the edge of the sleeves.

'It seems a bit incongruous,' Alice added. 'Do you know who it could be?'

Samantha looked at her before staring back down at the photograph. Alice also studied the long dark hair of the woman, her lips parted in a wide smile or possibly the start of a laugh, showing those two prominent front teeth. She noticed a slight gap in them now. The woman was painfully thin, oddly attractive. She appeared to be in a darkened pub, lit up by a flash.

'Never seen her before in my life,' said Samantha. She took the photo from her and peered at it more closely.

Alice swallowed, doing everything she could to retain her composure. Part of her wanted to be brutally honest, to ask Samantha if she'd ever seen a ghost – and part of her wanted to keep quiet. Instinctively, she kept quiet.

'It's not my predecessor?' Alice hardly knew where the question had come from.

'That girl? No, why did you think that?'

Alice shrugged. 'Just – it's a recent photo. Not sure why it's in this drawer.'

'I've no idea,' said Samantha, putting it down on the desk. She looked at the other papers. 'Oh look, you've found Forbes' diaries.'

She picked up the black book. 'These need looking after,' she said, as the strings on the spine's binding came apart. 'Bernard would love to take a look at these again. I'll take them up to show him.'

Before Alice could object – or rather, find a reason to object – Samantha had tucked the two books under her arm and was looking her in the face.

'It's getting snowy,' Samantha said, changing the subject.

Alice nodded. 'Have you ever been snowed in?'

'No, we're OK here. The lane gets slippery in the worst weather of course, but it's never been unnavigable. The trees keep it sheltered.'

'Well that's a good thing.'

'Yes. Bramley is wonderful, but you wouldn't want to be trapped here.'

Alice smiled, and looked down.

123

## 50

She took the journals!

Alice couldn't believe it. Samantha had, cool as ever, walked off with them.

Now she really was suspicious – and furious that the old woman had taken Forbes' books.

Once again feeling in a distracted fug, she decided to go outside for a walk to clear her head. She went into the kitchen and put on her anorak, scarf and boots.

The snow was starting to settle. Her footprints left black sludgy marks as she crossed the courtyard and headed back to the stumpery.

She examined again the narrow channel that George had dug. She dropped another stone down the gap, straining to hear the thud as it struck an unseen surface.

She stood up and looked around at the awkward stumps, the tall trees and shrubs around her, the matt sky. A snowflake caught her eyelash and she blinked. Her breath was steaming now.

Maybe it wasn't a cave at all.

She walked up the slope, leaving the last of the grotesque stumps behind. The holly became dense here, a mass of black and seaweed green. Prickly. But there was something about it that didn't seem quite right. It was all around chest height, as if... as if what?

As if it had all seeded at the same time.

Or been planted at the same time.

She walked along the edge of the holly, past two large chestnuts. At the end of the stumpery, there was a thick clump of coppiced hazel – again difficult to get through – and then another mass of holly, taller than the other patch. It looked like it had been there longer. Alice came around the side of that and once again climbed the bank, looping behind the impenetrable barrier of shrub. There were a few smooth rocks breaking out of the earth in places here, some patched with luminescent moss. She stepped over them, through an area of broken trees and scrub. And then suddenly she found the ground dipping, quite sharply.

She looked around. She was almost directly behind the thicket of holly. She imagined she would be in line with the centre of the stumpery below her. Ahead, there was a lip of rock and the trunks of several smooth green sycamore trunks snaking up from a scooped-out hollow. She stepped over the lip of the rock and began to descend into the hollow.

She stopped.

There, set into the bank beneath the holly, was some kind of indentation. Was it the mouth of a cave?

She almost tripped over herself, piling down the loose mass of twigs and bronze leaves that littered the bank. She reached the bottom and approached the opening.

As soon as she looked properly she saw that it wasn't an opening at all, just a sharp scoop out of the bank beneath the holly trees. She walked up to take a closer look.

At the top there was a stone ledge, supporting some of the scrub above. A few browny-gold roots had snaked over the top of it and back into the nutritious earth. Below the stone lip there was more loose earth, full of sticks, small stones and decomposing leaves, some yellow and dry, others black and mulchy. Alice stooped and climbed the soft bank towards the rock lip. She reached out with her gloved hands and pushed some of the soil and leaf matter away. Almost immediately she discovered something hard beneath it, more rock. As she pushed more of the earth away, she saw that the rock had an unusual smoothness to it. She dug harder, feeling like some kind of crazy terrier out in the cold.

The soil became more compacted, up against the rock. She realised she wouldn't be able to move it with her hands. It needed a spade, or even a digger. But there was something about the shaping of the stone she had discovered at the top. It was particularly… even.

Was it… could it be…

Was it a door?


## 51

As she returned through the Kitchen garden her phone bleated.

It was a text from Fran, apologising again for failing to do so many things and saying that she was in the area and would call in later that afternoon.

Within minutes of getting the message, Alice had formulated a list of the things she wanted to ask her boss. And, as she wove between the snow-piled vegetable plots, she realised she had one new request to make.


## 52

'Careful!'

Alice stretched back to try and catch Fran's arm as the RM lost her balance coming down the bank. She failed abysmally, and the large woman crashed down on to her backside, then slid through the mush to the bottom of the hollow.

'Are you OK?'

'Yes, yes,' said Fran with a gasp. She stood up, without taking Alice's proffered hand. She brushed the back of her khaki trousers and looked over towards the exposed section of rock, beneath the stony ledge. 'Interesting,' she said.

'Do you know if there's any record of a structure here?' said Alice.

'Not as far as I'm aware,' said Fran. 'Have you asked the S-Js?'

'No, not yet. I only found it this morning.'

'And you say George thinks there's a cave under here? That's why he was digging that trench?'

Alice nodded.

'How fascinating.'

'That's what I thought,' said Alice. She was itching to mention the woman and the boy who had led her out here in the middle of the night. *Itching*.

'I'd like to go get a couple of spades and start digging,' said Fran. 'But we'd better not.'

'Why not?' Alice had been thinking the same thing.

'Policy. We have to hand things like this straight over to the Trust professionals. We'd be in deep *merde* if we interfered with an archaeological site. Or worse, damaged it.'

They took a more careful look around the area for a while and then agreed to go and knock on the door of the S-J's quarters to see if they knew anything about it. As they headed back, Alice said:

'You weren't by any chance in town with Tom Gauge this morning, were you?'

'The farmer?'

'Yes.'

'Yes, yes I was. I met him for a coffee. He's been asking whether he can change the arrangements, now the Trust has taken over. He wants to buy the freehold of his farm. He's tired of renting.'

'Oh, right. I saw you in his car. I thought it was you, but then I thought it couldn't be.'

'Why?'

'Well, I thought you'd have arranged to see me if you were down in this neck of the woods. And then, well, you'd be in your own car, wouldn't you?'

'I have. Arranged to see you, haven't I?'

'Yes. After I texted.'

'I was going to pop in anyway. And I was in his car because we didn't think it was worth taking both our cars up to look at another parcel of the estate he wants to buy off us.'

'There's more to the estate?'

'A couple of isolated plots. Small ones. Aldermans is the main farm, which as you know runs along the northeast boundary of the estate. But there's – well, it's basically a large hill that has returned to woodland, and an area down by the river, which is pretty marshy. He wants to buy them off us and return them both to regular grazing.'

'But obviously he can't.'

'That's right. That lovely word at the core of the Trust's philosophy.'

'Inalienable,' said Alice.

'Yes. Ours forever!' Fran said, cackling like an evil overlord.

Alice laughed.

## 53

They were at the bottom of the stairs when they heard the sound.

It started as a vibration, a deep groan, a man's groan, rising in intensity and becoming a full-pitched wail. Alice thought she'd never heard anything so mournful in all her life. She looked at Fran and together they rushed up the stairs to the S-J's apartments. As they ran they heard another noise, also muffled through the walls, a crash.

Alice banged the apartment door with her fist.

The wailing stopped.

A few seconds later, Bernard opened the door to them. His mouth was hanging open, as if he couldn't believe they were there.

'Are you all right?' said Alice.

'What do you want?' he said.

'What was that noise?' said Fran.

'Nothing. I, err, knocked a table over, that's all. Had my drink on it.'

They all stood for a moment, staring at each other. Alice noticed Fran frown as she said:

'We think we've made a little discovery on the estate, Bernard. Might be nothing. We wondered if we could discuss it with you?'

'Discovery?'

Alice looked at the colour of his cheeks, how his whole face had sagged. She wondered about his health.

'Come in,' he said, beckoning them into the room. 'Have a seat. Samantha…' he began, then shouted her name towards the open door at the end of the living room: 'Sam! Sam, it's Fran and Alice. And I've knocked over my drink!' He looked searchingly back at them. 'Do you want a drink?'

Alice took her first proper look around at the room that was now the S-J's living room. It was a Solar room, a room to which the original families would have retreated when the entertaining and visitors became too much. It was double aspect, occupying the whole width of the house so looking over both the courtyard and the driveway that led away to the road. From studying the floorplans, Alice knew that the private study was beyond it, with a small corridor leading to the Master Bedroom, a second bedroom and a bathroom. Fran had told her that the study had been converted into a kitchen, so the S-Js didn't have to share the main kitchen with her. In Alice's mind's eye the long-term plan was to open the main kitchen to the public, and for her (or more likely her successor) to move into these quarters when the S-Js were too infirm to stay in Bramley.

Facing the main fireplace were two armchairs, one leather, faded to near-white on the arms, and the other maroon, so densely padded there hardly appeared room to sit in it. In between the chairs was an attractive Elizabethan oak strap casket, its top strewn with newspapers and magazines. Beside the leather chair, a spindly side table lay on its side, a tumbler upended beside it.

Alice picked up the glass whilst Fran righted the table. Samantha appeared at the far door.

'Is there a mess?' she said. She looked worried, resentful.

'Yes, spilt my whiskey,' said Bernard.

'It's only a small patch,' added Alice, surveying the faded rug. Persian, probably not too valuable. She spotted something else, a little further away on the floor – the black book, Forbes' journal, open with the pages fanning.

'Not again,' said Samantha, disappearing and coming back moments later with a cloth.

Alice saw her opportunity and took the cloth from her deftly. She knelt to wipe the rug. 'Are you sure you're OK, Bernard?' she said, looking up at him. 'We heard your cry downstairs,' she said slowly, 'then we heard the table crash.'

She looked up in time to see Samantha and Bernard exchange a glance. The old man's mouth was still hanging open.

Samantha broke the silence.

'I keep telling you, you need to see a doctor, Bernard.'

'I'm all right,' he replied. And then added: 'Yes, all right, I will…'

Samantha sat down in the padded chair. 'He has these headaches,' she said. 'But he refuses to see his GP.'

The seat of the leather armchair released a sigh – almost comical, like a whoopee cushion, Alice thought – as Bernard sunk down into it.

'Don't go on,' he said. 'What's this discovery, then?' he asked Fran, before turning around stiffly to Samantha and adding: 'Fran says they've discovered something.'

'What's that?' Samantha asked Fran, who was now standing facing them, with her back to the empty fireplace.

Alice stretched out and picked up the journal, taking a long glance at one of the open pages before shutting it.

*The Lion Man appears to have links to Chronos, to some form of Time function. Replays Time? Most fascinating of the Mithras figures… Like Bramley's –*

'Alice found it,' said Fran, and Alice looked up. 'Or rather, it might have been George first. He found a hole in the ground, near the stumpery. He took it on himself to dig it out a bit. Then Alice found a hollow further up, with what might be a buried doorway.'

'A doorway?' said Samantha. 'How bizarre.'

'Yes. You don't know anything about a cave or old structure in the grounds do you?' said Fran.

Alice straightened up and set the book back on the table, at the same time catching Samantha's aghast glance at her husband. Which, of course, was not unusual – aghast or disgusted was how she looked most of the time.

'No,' said Bernard.

'Do you mind if we arrange a survey?' said Fran. 'Get a Trust archaeologist down?'

'What will they do?' said Samantha.

'At first, nothing more than a look around the site. If they think it's a structure, they'll probably want to do some preliminary excavations.'

'You want to dig up Bramley?' said Samantha.

'Potentially,' said Fran.

'It's fine, dear,' said Bernard to his wife. 'There won't be anything there.'

Gazing at his face, in the cold light coming in through the high leaded windows, Alice thought Bernard himself looked anything but fine. In fact, with his blotchy cheeks and hangdog jaw, he reminded her of her mother in the bad old days, dazed and confused.

Or of someone who had just seen a ghost.

When it became clear that Fran could not provide her with any more of the support Alice needed, it was not difficult to get her to agree to her next request: a long weekend away.

Alice's contract stated that she must spend at least eighty percent of her time at Bramley, primarily for security purposes but also as she understood to send a clear message to the S-Js about the change of circumstances. Whilst she would never normally have asked for a couple of days leave only a few weeks into a new job, Fran agreed that, with the barriers to making any more meaningful progress, it made sense. Alice said she would happily work over the holiday period if need be.

'You can't work over Christmas!' said Fran. 'You must want to spend time with your family – and your boyfriend?' She picked up another of the ginger cookies she'd brought and took a bite.

'The boyfriend is over,' said Alice. She thought about how so much had got in the way of her speaking to Fran about the reason – and now it felt too late. Or was that just an excuse? God, she could almost hate herself sometimes. 'And my close family are all – passed away,' she added.

'Oh, I am sorry,' said Fran.

'Yes. I'm alone in the world.'

It was meant to be a light-hearted quip but as soon as she said it Alice could feel a heaviness in the air. Fran stopped chewing her cookie.

'It's just a joke,' said Alice. Then added, a little too quickly: 'I didn't mean it like that. To sound so sad…'

'Well, that does remind me,' said Fran, resuming her chomping, 'that I need to get down details of your next... of who to contact in an emergency.'

Alice thought. 'That's a tricky one. My closest relatives are distant – both in relationship and geography. My relationship with Matthew – my boyfriend – finished almost as soon as it started.'

'What about friends?'

'Let me think about it.'

'OK. No hurry. I'll ask you next time. I just need someone to put down on the form.'

'I guess my lack of dependents – and responsibilities – is helpful for a job like this.'

Fran smiled. 'Yes, I guess it is,' she said.

'One other thing,' said Alice.

'Yes?'

'How long did the Trust negotiate with the S-Js before they agreed to the transfer?'

'A long time. Why?'

'I found a letter from one of our solicitors from nine years back, outlining Heads of Terms.'

'Yes, I wasn't with the Trust then. But when my boss – His Highness, John Bletchley – briefed me on the background, he told me that the first phase of discussions reached a hiatus.'

'Why was that?'

'Apparently some investments they had in a Brazilian oil company produced a massive turnaround for their finances. It was a major surprise to everyone, I'm not sure even if the S-Js knew they had the investment when their accountant told them. But – well, as you can see, it only delayed the inevitable.'

Alice nodded.

'Anyhows, where are you planning to go on your mini-break?' said Fran.

'The Lakes. There's this tiny caravan I go up to, let by this woman who lives in one of the valleys.'

'Sounds lovely.'

'Yes. It is.'

# The Message

## 55

As Alice drove north, up the M6 towards the Lake District, she remembered a horror novel she had read once.

She recalled how the narrator, an author who hadn't been able to write since his wife's death, made a striking analogy about how the process of writing worked. For him, it wasn't about a conscious, focused effort – initially at least. It was about letting the guys in the cellar do their work. He would go about his life without any great expectations whilst those guys – his subconscious – worked out the plot and the details of the storyline for him.

Now, Alice decided, she was going to do a little of that herself. When she'd told Fran she wanted a break, she had been planning to go carefully through everything that had happened since she'd arrived at Bramley, perhaps even lay out a few post-it notes on a table, to try and work out what might be going on. But, seeing the sun lighting the hills and fields and leafless trees on either side of the traffic-clogged motorway, she decided she would have none of that. Instead she would let it all go and concentrate on relaxing and enjoying herself. She would see whether the guys in the cellar decided to throw up any clues without interference from her.

She had set off early, so despite the poor motorway traffic she reached the lovely Troutbeck valley in time for a late lunch in a toasty old pub, heated through by a wood fire. She spent some time talking to an old boy who was lamenting the loss of a local quarry a few years back. He wore a huge pair of bifocal glasses that magnified his rheumy eyes and he sat at the bar sipping a half-pint of Jennings and eating pork scratchings. He became wary of her when she told him she worked for the Trust for England, telling her he considered them little more than 'a bunch of bandits' making corrupt deals with landowners. But she realised quickly that he didn't have any evidence for that apart from something his father had told him way back in the 1970s, and he wasn't at all intent on making an enemy of her. In fact, she felt that like many old timers, he expressed his opinions more out of habit than conviction, realising as he did so that he was perverting the easy course of a conversation he wished to continue. So at the end of his set-piece she made a light-hearted quip about all big institutions having their dodgy sides, which enabled them to finish with an amicable discussion about his days as a quarryman, mining the beautiful green slate they used locally for roofing and graves.

When she came out of the hot pub the wind was bitter, surging down the valley from Kirkstone Pass where all that was left of the man's quarry was a series of quiet grey slashes in the mountain sward.

June Waverley's cottage was accessed via a farm road that snaked up the hillside, crisscrossing a gushing brook. On one side, the road was edged by a pristine drystone wall. As her Fiat laboured up the gradient, the views Alice glimpsed through the gates in the wall were stunning, great expanses of grassland billowing up towards the sharp, tree-lined edge of the hill opposite. The shapely humps of grass were called drumlins, she remembered from her Geography at school. Formed by ice age glaciers that crushed everything in their path.

June had an uncanny ability of being out in her garden waiting for her whenever she arrived. She was an energetic woman on the far side of middle age, who always managed to make Alice feel indecisive and compromised, like she wasn't living her life fully enough. There she was now, digging over a flower bed in front of her cottage despite the freezing cold. Alice drove into the small drive and switched off the engine.

'Thought you might not remember which one it was,' said the woman as Alice got out. Alice was sure she said that every time she came.

*I should text mum back.*

On the verge of saying hello, the thought popped unbidden into Alice's mind. The guys in the cellar doing their job.

'Hi June,' she said. 'You don't have to wait out for me, I know where you are now.'

'Well, just in case,' said the woman. 'Like some tea? I've baked a cake, a Victoria sponge.'

'Wonderful.'

It was a good hour before they'd finished chatting in June's kitchen. When Alice finally collected her pack from the car and took it around the rear of the cottage to the permanently stowed caravan it was nearly dark. The wind had died, but the air was icy cold, fingering at all the weakest points in her outfit. The caravan however, like the pub, was roasting, heated by three electric radiators. Alice's first job was to turn them all off and strip down to her T-shirt and khaki trousers.

Then she sat down at the tiny dining table and pulled out her phone. The signal was low. She wondered, did you need a signal if you were texting the dead?

She stifled a desire to giggle and typed:

*Hi Mum, I love you. Can you tell me anything else about Bramley?*

As soon as she pushed send the phone pinged with a new message. It was from her mum.

*red r bboo K luv to !*

What did that mean? *Luv to* seemed simple enough. Love you too. Her eyes felt hot. She realised she was sweating. She would have opened the window if a part of her didn't feel so guilty about wasting all that heat. She looked out at the dark blue courtyard, the side of June's house. A cat appeared, crouching low in its rush towards the cat flap.

She was communicating with her dead mother by text. Alice had to remind herself of that for fear she would turn into a gibbering wreck, face-to-face with the incomprehensible.

redrbbook. Red book. Reader book. Read a book. Read the book.

*Do you mean Forbes' book?*

The response this time was simple.

*yis*

OK, so there was more to the book and Forbes. Perhaps he held the key to the mystery of Bramley.

There was something more she needed to know. She wasn't scared of ghosts. In fact, the paranormal activities in Bramley had removed her underlying anxieties by giving her something to focus on. But she knew that the stories *behind* ghosts could well be scary.

*Am I in danger, Mum?* she typed.

## 58

She woke the next morning to the sound of... nothing.

The profound peacefulness of the valley reminded her of her first night in Bramley, when she had slept so well before the mysteries had become apparent. There was something so powerful, so rich and replenishing, to be found far from the perpetual busyness of even the smallest towns and villages.

She lifted her phone from the tight gap between the mattress and the bedframe where she'd stashed it.

Still no reply.

Maybe that was it from her mum. Still, at least she had her lead. She needed to find a way to read more of Forbes' journal.

But for now, the hills.

She didn't feel like breakfast so made herself a simple cheese and pickle sandwich from the supplies she'd picked up in Windermere on the way through. She filled a water bottle and stuffed them both in her backpack with a banana, and then she was off.

Alice didn't need her car. She walked straight out of June's garden and up the road for quarter of a mile to a stile that gave access to a boggy landscape of sheep and sedge-locked hillocks. Within an hour she was at the ridge, looking across towards the most heavily mythologised Lakes (as she considered them), Grasmere and Rydal Water, where Wordsworth had lived. She could either turn south and walk down the ridge to the superlative views of Windermere from Wansfell Pike, or head further up the valley in the direction of Kirkstone. She decided on the latter.

Walking on top of the world, for a good time, was the best way of releasing new thoughts. There were a few brief squalls of rain. As they cleared she felt her spirits buoying, watching the furrowed brow of green studded with rocks that rose before her. She expected the 'boys down below' to start giving her insight into Bramley, but instead she began to wonder at the course of her life, how it had seemingly without any intention of her own led her to this point where she was so… alone. She didn't have any family to speak of, Uncle Bob could hardly be thought of even as a relative in Australia. Her best friends at school were gone, one a psychopathic turncoat, the other now happily married and absorbed into an idyllic life in Switzerland, to all effects entirely lost to her. She had had a few friends at University, but Stirling was a long way away from Farnborough and now, a few years after leaving, they hardly ever contacted each other. A late developer, Alice had for a while considered setting up a Facebook account – or, even more challenging, an Instagram one – to try and re-establish some contacts, but in the end had never found time for it. Which, she knew, had really meant she was not that into it. Social media – outside of its necessary uses at work – was just not her thing.

Her thoughts of Matthew started with his physical presence, his beautiful face and (almost) perfect six-pack. She liked him, he could make her laugh and he was sophisticated and cultured. But, as with all men, a part of her had always remained distant from him. Thinking back, she realised she had clocked his attraction at Albany Park quite early on. It had been flattering, she had enjoyed the attention after such a long period with none. But the way things had panned out at Bramley, the incidents with George and Samantha, Matthew's reaction when she told him about the ghosts and the texts – hadn't she secretly been happy that all that had driven a wedge between them, before anything deep could start to develop?

Didn't she just want to be alone? Wasn't that why the job at Bramley had appealed to her so much when she saw it that Saturday morning in the *Farnborough Advertiser*? It was the chance to do something truly on her own, to make a mark solely using her own skills and abilities. It was the opportunity to do something that wouldn't be down to anybody else, not some man (or possibly woman) who would ultimately claim the credit.

That was what drove her. She was not as quiet and distant as she thought. She wanted to make an impact.

In her own way, she was competitive. Fran had made light of the Trust for England's inalienable ownership of British heritage. But now she could see it. She, Alice Deaton, was going to work out a way to reflect Bramley's appeal – its unique, ineffable character – for everyone who was interested in seeing or studying it.

Looking up, she could see the clouds lightening towards the horizon, towards the start of the Kirkstone Pass. It was going to be a good day's walking, she thought. She had an obscure, but very special, future before her. One day she would be married with kids – but not for a long time. A very long time. There was plenty to do before then.

For a moment she thought there was a bird nearby, perhaps a skylark, releasing its high-pitched tweets of joy above the moors. Then she realised that she was being stupid, there would be no skylarks up in the air at this time of year. They would be hunkered down, or more likely migrated to some hot country near the Equator.

No, the noise she had heard was the sound of her phone, collecting a message from the empty ether on this bleak windy mountainside.

She drew it out of her windcheater pocket and checked the message.

It was one word, received from her mum:

*yES ;!*

It was the last she ever heard from her.

143

*Bramley's Secret*

59

She arrived back at Bramley late on the Tuesday evening, her wipers struggling to clear the sleet blotting her windscreen. Alice had been planning to stay an extra night and walk on the Wednesday, but the forecast was just getting worse and she didn't (a) want to walk in snow and (b) have to drive back through it.

She pulled up in the drive and killed the engine. For a moment she savoured the heat, realising she wouldn't be this warm again until the next time she was back in the car. Then she pulled on her waterproof, collected the keys from the glove compartment, and lifted her pack from the passenger seat. She took a deep breath, then opened the door and climbed out, using her phone torch to hurry through the icy sludge across the bridge and up to Bramley's giant oak gate. She took the iron key from her pocket and, after a bit of wrestling about, suddenly realised that it was open. The S-Js must have forgotten to lock up! She remembered the first time she had used that key, locking the door after Fran had left. How much had happened since then… She felt like she had lived another life.

Dimensionality. Layers of experience, bedding down across themselves like rich rock strata. That's what life was all about. Her mum had told her she was in danger.

144

But still she had come back. The alternative, to give up, go find another job, was too banal. And after all, when it all boiled down to basics, she had one of Britain's greatest institutions backing her up in the real, physical world. And from her own experience, the supernatural world worked only in a moral dimension, helping to right wrongs. Look at Susannah and Charlotte's gran.

But – she mentally promised her mum, as she crossed the slushy cobbles of the courtyard – she would take extra care. Extra, extra care, as she used to promise, when she was a child and allowed to go out to the park alone.

She looked up, blinking against the cold wet, and was surprised to see a light on in the Solar Room of the S-J's quarters. It was after midnight and they were normally in bed earlier, by eleven at the latest. She let herself into the main building and headed up to her freezing bedroom. She reached her door and fished in her pocket for the key – then, with a sinking feeling, realised she had left it in the car.

Ever since she'd lost a master key for Albany Park, resulting in a locksmith having to drill the front door at great expense, she'd been paranoid about keys. When she was walking in the Lakes she had taken the main keys to the house off her keyring and stored them in the glove compartment of the car to make sure she didn't lose them on some wild and lonely moor. When she'd got out of the car she must have left the small key to her room behind.

Cursing, she made her way back down across the courtyard, unlocked the gate again, and crossed the bridge to the drive. She opened the passenger door and felt in the glove compartment. Good – her paranoia passed – the key was there. She put it her pocket – and then heard a noise.

It was a soft humming sound, broken by an intermittent, harsher tone, coming from the darkness beyond the manor, in the direction of the gardens. Instinctively, she shook her phone to kill the torch. She crouched behind the car and listened as the noises grew louder and finally took on the resonance of human voices – a man, another, higher-pitched man, and probably a woman. Alice heard the crunch of feet as they reached the weedy gravel surrounding the moat wall.

The sleet was savaging her cheeks. She peered into the darkness that just would not give. But she could hear – hear the sound of an old woman's enunciation, a rasping tone as if she (Samantha, it was Samantha of course) had a throat infection. And hear the deeper, landed-gentry tone of Bernard's response – and then the other, higher voice, a man's voice, but one she was sure she had never heard before.

She strained to hear what they were saying. But try as she might, they were just too far away, or more likely the sleet was too muffling, for her to make out their words. She heard the gate open – she was so glad she had forgotten her key, otherwise they would have found it locked – and then the sound of the three of them disappearing into the old house.

What were the S-Js doing out at this time, in such atrocious weather? Did they have a death wish? They weren't exactly spring chickens. And who on earth was that with them?

She looked around but there were no other cars beside the Aston Martin in the parking area. Then, without lighting her torch, she made her way carefully back to the main gate. They had locked the door and she wondered whether she should leave it a while before she went through, but quickly decided it was too damned cold for that, so unlocked it again. She went in, locked up, and headed across the forecourt towards the Great Hall doorway. She looked up at the S-J's quarters. The light was still on, but she couldn't see anyone in the window. She half-considered hanging around just in case their guest appeared. But it was bitter and what would they think if they looked out the window and saw her standing there in the sleet, spying up on them?

She hurried into the building. As she stepped inside, into the darkness of the hall, she realised that when she went out first time she had probably – *probably*, she couldn't be sure – left the hall light on. Would that have made them realise she was back? Or would they have thought nothing of it, thinking they'd left it on themselves? She didn't know. Then, as she lit her torch, she saw their wet footprints on the floor. What about her own prints? How well had she wiped her feet on the mat when she came in? Would they have seen them? They were expecting her back the next day. But surely it didn't matter to them one way or the other whether she was in or not?

She had this gut instinct that they were doing what they were doing *because* she was supposed to be away. Which made her want to keep her presence here now secret. She would rather they found out about her being back in the morning, in the light of day.

Then she had an idea. Instead of going up the nearest stairs by the kitchen, which emerged right beside the S-J's apartment, she went through the crypt – using her torch again, so as not to turn on any lights – and then headed up the east wing stairwell. As she reached the top of those stairs – the one the ghost boy had disappeared down on her first day – she turned off her torch and went to the large windows that looked across the courtyard to the S-J's rooms.

She saw the winey glow of the lights in the diamond-paned windows, lighting the dark sleet that fell down across them. And she could – just – make out two figures in there, both probably men. There was something about the shape of the first, his hunched shoulders, that made her sure it was Bernard. And he was moving near, talking to, another man, taller, light-haired no, he had a hat on, a grey hat? Both he and Bernard seemed to be wearing long coats, probably macs.

Hopeless. They were too far away. She cursed, wishing her eyesight were better, or that the sleet would let off for just a moment.

And then Samantha appeared, her face right up against the window, and looked straight across the courtyard towards her.

Alice froze.

As the old woman remained there, she sank slowly down below the window frame.

Could she have been seen?

Surely not, it was too dark. There was no light source behind her. All Samantha would have seen was the sleet, reflecting the light as it swirled past her window.

Surely.

Feeling the shadow of paranoia again, Alice decided to cease her spying. She was exhausted from the long day, the drive, and now this. She needed sleep.

She crept quietly down the landing to her room, took out her key, and let herself in.

She put the door on the latch as soon as she was inside. Quickly, she turned on her heater, dug around in her backpack for her sleeping T-shirt, tracksuit bottoms, and woolly socks and buried herself under the ice block of her bedding.

She imagined this latest intrigue would keep her awake thinking, but within moments she was asleep.

60

But she slept poorly.

There was a recurrent dream about a masked man, bent over double and creeping through the woods, that she kept waking from and then slumping back into. She remembered someone moaning, a man by a post box, bats in the air, a woman with a calculator.

When she woke the next morning, images from the dream flittered about her mind like dark butterflies. She discarded most of it as meaningless nonsense, fuelled by her recent worries – but not the moaning.

The latter was not part of the dream. She knew it. She was sure it was something she had heard in the night. She was sure, in fact, that she knew what it was.

Bernard, wailing like a lost soul, just like before.

When she walked out later into the icy morning, she wished she had set her alarm and waited to see who the S-J's guest was when he left. She could have got herself a pot of coffee and sat watching discretely from the library window for when he came out. But after the disturbed night's sleep, punctuated by Bernard's wail, she had ended up oversleeping. Now, she knew there were things she should be doing about her work, despite the lack of support from Fran. But more urgently she felt she had to do whatever she could to get to the bottom of the house's secrets. How could they open to the public with all this – whatever *this* really was – going on?

She got in her car and started the engine after three attempts. She drove out of Bramley and used the satnav app on her phone to navigate the lanes until she came to a dishevelled drystone wall, broken by a solitary drive. The drive led through a small dark pine plantation to a farmhouse, with several barns and outbuildings. From the elevated position of the road she could see a Land Rover and a couple of other cars, a brown Ford and some kind of dilapidated sports car, a Midget or a Triumph Spitfire perhaps.

She didn't want to go in, but instead contented herself with the painted sign that was fixed to the wall – Aldermans. The homemade sign had slipped slightly, and there was a splat of bird shit across the middle, but at least she knew now where Tom, her nearest neighbour, lived. She might be being overcautious, but now she had found her safe house should she for any reason need it. She wasn't going to forget in a hurry that her mum had texted her from beyond the grave to tell her she was in danger.

The engine idling, she looked to the opposite side of the road, where bleak, ice-patched fields rose gently to a low brow, the field that she now calculated was the one containing the bull. Beyond that would be the wood, dipping down into Bramley and its gardens.

She wondered briefly if the bull were kept outside through the whole winter.

The bull…

## 61

Next she drove to town where she parked herself in Doodley's, a café on the high street. She ordered scrambled eggs on toast and, with a nice full signal, began to search on her phone.

*Bramley house people*

First came several copies of the same photo of Bernard and Samantha, posing at the head of the bridge with the flaky cream walls of the house behind them. Bernard had an arm rested on Samantha's shoulder and was smiling broadly, showing his teeth. The wind had caught Samantha's hair and she was holding it down, looking slightly off to the right of camera. The signs of age so apparent in them now were not there.

It was a photograph taken for a country life magazine, one Alice had never heard of. The story was from 2011 and included three shots from the interior. The house appeared in a far better state then, or at least the Great Hall, Squire's Room and Solace Room that featured.

Flicking down the search page, Alice saw a few more photos of the S-Js, alone and together. All were even further back in time; there were none since the 2011 picture. There was one with Bernard shooting in woods with a group of men; another with him sitting writing at the desk in the study, the colours faded as if it were taken in the 1970s or '80s. Then there was one of Samantha talking to a man in a Barbour, who it seemed from the caption was the Chairman of the county's Wildlife Trust. It was from an article in the Wildlife Trust's magazine, about how the organisation was encouraging responsible landowners to engage with conservation measures.

So one saves wildlife while the other one shoots it, mused Alice.

There cropped up a few images of the former residents of the house. Alice found photos of Bernard's parents, Samantha's mother, and Bernard's grand- and great-grand-parents. There were a few paintings of other ancestors – a merchant banker from the 1930s, a family portrait with dogs and horses in the late nineteenth-century, a tall, elegant drawing of a woman in a 1920s Charleston-style dress and hat, standing beside a table with a lamp.

But no photos, as she had hoped, of Forbes.

Her scrambled eggs arrived and she set her phone aside whilst she wolfed them down. She was starving!

Then she asked for a refill of coffee and searched *Bramley House Forbes* but nothing relevant came up. She tried a few variations – *Bramley Forbes, Bramley Forbes Italy, Forbes Ostia Antica, Forbes excavation Ostia* – but almost every search was dominated by Forbes banking entries, or an obscure Victorian painter called Forbes, or somewhere called Bramley Village. Nothing related to her man.

She checked her data and found it was low. She gestured to the waitress and was about to settle up when she had another random idea. She typed:

*Jerry Bramley garden*

As she scrolled down she wasn't surprised to be disappointed. There were old black and white pictures of Bramley Road in Kensington, pictures of formal gardens, a photo of a rosy apple. She was about to exit the search when her eye was caught by a more natural, appealing shot of a woman in a garden. The woman had an arm out towards the photographer and was turning away, laughing.

Alice read the title:

*With Jerry in Bramly garden*

She felt her hand shaking as she clicked on the image.

It was an Instagram profile, *@marystevensgoodtimes*, with only two photos.

The first was this one. The woman turning away from the photographer had long dark hair, a gaunt complexion. She was wearing a long flowery dress. Her hand was thrust palm open towards the camera and she was half in profile, Alice could see the angular side of her cheek, the corner of her laughing mouth.

It was when she looked at the other photo that her heart felt like it had burst in her chest.

It was a profile shot of the ghost woman.


62


The woman was smiling, showing her large front teeth with the gap. She looked happy, but had an air of being slightly ill, emaciated. The skin around her dark, shiny eyes was pinkish-purple, as if she had eczema. Or an illness. Or a drug habit.

Looking good babe, said a comment.

'Here's your bill, love.'


153

She looked up to see the waitress, a young woman with short green-dyed hair, place the slip of paper on her table.

'Oh, thanks,' she said.

She checked the details of the account. Two followers, both of whose accounts she found were closed. Five following, both of the closed accounts and three bands, all heavy metal. The dates on the photos were from nine years ago, when Instagram could have only just started. There was only one *like* on each of them, from *@rachelbelle1258*, one of the closed accounts. She had also posted the comment on the facial shot.

She googled *Mary Stevens* and *marystevensgoodtime* but there were thousands if not millions of Mary Stevens.

Jerry. Fran had said that the gardener before George was called Jerry. Could this be his wife or partner? Was this the man Alice had seen in that weird memory she'd shared with the ghost, chasing her through the house? Chasing her in fun – before the distant splashing sound?


## 63


Her mind was a riot as she drove back to Bramley, wondering who had been in the house last night with the S-Js, and who the woman might be.

And more importantly, how the woman had died. Because died she certainly had. As yet Alice knew of no other ways she could have turned into a ghost, she thought, the corners of her lips twitching in a half smile.

Did Bramley have a dark – properly dark – history? Had there been a killer in the house?

She thought about whether she should involve the police. But what would she tell them? I've been seeing a ghost of this woman on Instagram and wonder whether she might have been murdered? She could imagine the expression on the officer's face.

As she drove, the weather mimicked the storm in her mind with a blur of snowflakes, flying up at her windscreen as fast as the wipers could clear them. Looking around at the trees and fields she could tell that this time it was going to settle.

She really didn't want to be snowed in at Bramley. Not under these circumstances.

The sky was a filthy grey-brown as she entered the driveway at Bramley. The snow had all but erased the ground. The roofs of the old building were layering up like icing, and thin trails of snow scored the transoms of the windows. She imagined a freeze on the moat that night and thought about how exciting it would be to walk or even skate along it in the morning.

As she walked through to the courtyard she glanced up at the S-J's lit windows. For a moment she felt a sliver of guilt, making two elderly folk sit in their poorly heated apartments without being allowed to light a fire, as they would have done only a year or so ago. Still, there was nothing she could do about it.

Inside, she headed upstairs to her room. As she passed the S-J's rooms, she heard a click behind her and turned to see Samantha standing in the door.

'I thought I heard you,' said the old woman.

'Looking bleak outside,' said Alice.

'Yes. That's what I was going to say. Bernard and I hate the cold and he's not feeling at all well, so we're going to go away for a day or two.'

'Oh, OK.'
'You'll be on your own here, I hope you don't mind.'
'No, not at all.'
'Good.'

## 64

In some ways, it was the perfect piece of news.

Alice wasn't certain, but she was pretty sure her master set of keys included one for their apartment. As the property manager, she needed to be able to access all areas for health and safety reasons, if none other. Whilst she didn't like the idea of snooping, she knew she had to get to the bottom of the house's mystery. And – following her mum's text – Forbes' book was the most likely thing to hold the key.

She just hoped the S-Js wouldn't second guess her and take it with them.

Now, she needed to find something to keep her mind occupied for the rest of the afternoon while she waited for them to go.

She decided to make a start with some of the tidying and cleaning that needed doing. She had been holding off on this, thinking it would be a good job to get the volunteers involved with. But right now it was just the kind of work she needed, engaging but not demanding.

Fran had told her the S-J's had given permission for her to make a start on the Squire's room, so she spent the next three hours in there, sorting through bric-a-brac that at times she had no idea whether it was worthless or priceless – although she guessed that, with his forensic knowledge of the house's chattels, Bernard wouldn't have neglected anything of value. She wondered in passing how much of Bramley's heritage he and Samantha had sold to keep things going as long as possible on their own.

Every available surface in the room – settees, window ledges, chairs, tables, the mantelpiece, even the ornate radiator boxes – was littered with *stuff*. She sorted books, cigarette cases, playing cards, candlesticks, ornaments, clocks, vases, pen holders, letter openers, newspapers, drink mats, soda bottles and canisters, spectacles, whisky tumblers, lamps, board games, photographs (none of any help) and much, much more. She put things into piles, which she marked up with handwritten post-it notes. One for future display, which included items that she considered of charm, like a rosewood pipe and tobacco tin that still had the whiff of an era about them. One for possible display, with question marks on items that could add to interpretation stories or seasonal / one-off themes, like the Halloween idea she'd had when she saw the witch marks in the Great Hall. Then there was a pile for things she considered mundane but reckoned should be checked by an archivist or someone else in the Trust for heritage value. And finally, there was the pile she thought that, after a perfunctory check by the archivist, could be either thrown away or stored in a basement somewhere, depending on the Trust's policy.

She hadn't been looking forward to the tidy but when she saw the main door by the Great Hall swing open she glanced at her watch and realised it was nearly four o'clock. Outside it was gloomy, darkness wasn't far away. The snow had stopped but it had settled neatly in the courtyard, eliminating the cobbles with a knobbly covering of white.

She watched as Samantha and Bernard emerged from the doorway with their bags, Henry bouncing black and happy in the snow. The Labrador plunged his snout down and shoved a powdery spray into the air, snapping ineffectually as it showered back to the ground. Whilst Alice couldn't hear anything they said, the S-Js looked stressed and anxious. The fierceness with which Samantha turned to Bernard suggested an argument in progress. Alice noticed he still had the remnants of his hangdog expression, as if he hadn't managed to get much sleep.

The old couple made their way slowly across the courtyard, breaking the pristine snow. Samantha threw a glance back at the upper wing, towards Alice's room, before they disappeared under the covered walkway from yard to gate.

They were gone!

Alice resisted the urge to run straight up and try their door. She would give them a while, make sure the car started and they hadn't forgotten anything that would bring them back. In fact, she would give them a good long time, wait until after she'd had her dinner.

Better safe than sorry. She resumed her tidying, but her mind was far away from it now.

65

Later that night, she headed down the landing to their apartment.

Outside the great windows, moonlight was penetrating the thin cloud cover, giving a faint, ethereal glow to the snow-covered roofs and courtyard. Alice could see her features reflected in the small, wonky panes of glass, a fractal ghost-self staring back at her. For a moment she felt the full weight, the strangeness, of her situation. Of being on her own, for the first time, in this ancient, mysterious place. This ancient, mysterious, *haunted* place. It quickened her pulse, and she tried not to think about it, distracting herself with the task in hand.

And what a task. She was on the verge of committing an activity which, whilst not strictly criminal, was nevertheless highly unethical. Breaking into – albeit with a key – someone's rooms, searching through their personal things. If her fifteen-year-old self could see her now…

Still, needs must, as her dad always said. Irritatingly.

She reached the S-J's door and drew out the master keys. They were held on a massive ring, probably a copper bracelet in fact. They ranged from tiny padlock keys to giant iron ones for the old doors. In the midst were a dozen or so Yale keys, differing shades of brown, bronze and silver. She began to try these out, one by one. With the third, the latch turned. A small shove, and the door was open.

She was in.

She felt a moment's concern about switching on the lights. Supposing Bernard and Samantha came back? If the lights were on they would know she was there as soon as they entered the courtyard. At least if the lights weren't on and she heard them coming she'd have time to put things back and escape.

But really, what was the chance of them returning now?

In the end she switched on one of the small reading lamps. They could easily have forgotten to turn off one of those.

She began to search the room.

The first thing she realised was – should, after all her work in the house, it still need confirming – the S-Js really were messy. Nothing was put away and nothing was dusted or hoovered. Unwashed cups of tea and spirit tumblers fought for space amongst magazines (Alice noted the irony of copies of *Good Housekeeping*) and yellowing copies of the *Telegraph*. A stale, half-eaten piece of cake, Battenberg, rested on a saucer by a whiskey glass. The mantelpiece above the fireplace was thick with dust, broken by pens, vases and other paraphernalia stacked between two china dogs and a pricey-looking Art Deco clock of ebony and lemon wood. Alice noticed a rectangular sliver on the mantelpiece where the dust wasn't quite so thick – as if it had only not been dusted for weeks instead of years.

She didn't feel at all comfortable as she poked around. Thankfully it didn't take her long to find the first of Forbes' books, on top of the magazines beside Bernard's armchair. Shortly after, she came across the second, placed upright on the windowsill. She decided she would take them away and read them in her own room, then bring them back later.

As she was leaving, she noticed a piece of cloth over the back of one of the Elizabethan weaved chairs in the corner, by a small TV. Curious, she went over and lifted it up.

It was a soft cotton cap, beige-coloured, and tapering towards a slightly thicker top. As she lifted it, the top folded over and she realised what it was – a Phrygian cap, like the French revolutionaries used to wear.

And like Mithras was wearing, on the tapestry she cleaned.

She stood in the soft lamplight of the dirty room and looked out at the darkness, once again catching her ghost-self in reflection.

Who was that person with the S-Js last night, that man with the dark hair…?

Alongside this hat, he had been wearing an unshapely coat, she remembered.

More like a robe.

On instinct, instead of leaving the quarters, she strode quickly across to the other door. Forgetting about her concerns, she turned on the lights and made a quick search of the S-J's kitchen – dirty plates smeared with a brown-edged cream sauce still on the table – bathroom, and finally the bedrooms, checking the wardrobes and drawers. But she found nothing significant, nothing beyond the fusty old-fashioned clothing of people from a smarter, almost vanished, era.

She was leaving the master bedroom when she noticed a small side drawer in the table beside one of the two single beds. The copy of a Mary Wesley novel on the table made her guess it was Samantha's bed. She went and tugged on the handle of the drawer, easing it out.

Inside there was an old packet of cigarettes, Winston's, open but with the cellophane wrapper left on. There were a few other odds and sods, a lighter, pen, some reading glasses – and a photo in a frame. Alice picked it up and looked at it. There was no doubt about the identity of the young man in the picture with the black curly hair, smoking a cigarette on a bench in the garden.

'George…'

Why did Samantha have a picture of the gardener in her bedside drawer? How infinitely, infinitely strange.

Baffled, Alice replaced the picture. She went back into the Solar room, turned off the lights and left the apartment.

She headed back to her room to read.


## 66

She woke up on her sofa, cold, the reading lamp on, the windows blank with dark.

Forbes' book, the weird, esoteric one, was open on her lap.

Her back was aching from the slouched position her body had sunk into after she must have passed out. She looked at the time − 2.17 − and then again at the last passage she had been reading. Again − and again.

*It is a narrow Cavern some forty feet long, with a concave brick Roof. There is some stone Furniture within, a long Table and Benches around which I suspect dining was partaken. There appears to be a narrow opening in the Roof, now filled in with Earth from the Mound above. From my Readings, there is speculation by Archaeologists that this would have served for the Tauroctony. There is no doubt in my Mind that the Structure which I have uncovered in the Grounds is a fine Example of an Ancient Mithraeum, constructed when the Legionaries were in Britain in the Second or Third Century…*

Her thoughts returned to where they had left off before she fell asleep.

Was Forbes referring to the structure in the stumpery? Could there be an ancient Mithras temple buried in Bramley's garden? It was hard to imagine Bramley's heritage being any richer than it already was – but, if this were true, it would surely make it one of the biggest jewels in the Trust for England's crown!

She could barely wait to speak to Fran about it. She would call her first thing in the morning.

Was she ever going to get back to sleep? She had dropped off from exhaustion, but now her mind was racing furiously once again. She stood up, turned away from the sorry fireplace, towards her bed…

And screamed.


67


On all fours, on her bed, the ghost woman crouched.

'What the…!' Alice cried.

The woman's long black hair hung down around her pale face. She was arching her back like some kind of succubus, vampish, predatorial. She stared at Alice, rocking backwards and forwards on her hips and shoulders. After the Instagram photo, Alice now noticed the pinkness around her eyes, which before had merged into shadow. The woman opened her mouth, her large white incisors showing.

'What – what do you want?' said Alice.

The woman shook her face, her hair swinging beside it. She looked full of irritation – or loathing.

Alice took a deep breath.

'I can't help you – I can't do anything – unless you let me know what it is you want.'

The woman tilted her head, studying Alice's face carefully. Like a dog trying to understand its owner.

'I saw your account. Your Instagram photos. I saw that note, about being in the garden here, with Jerry. Who was he, who was Jerry?'

Slowly, the woman shook her head. Her gaze felt to Alice like a knife, not a slashing dagger but a poniard, a nail-like blade designed to push through a knight's visor. She looked like… like a *murderer*.

'Is – is the boy anything to do with you?'

The woman closed her eyes. Alice's mind threatened to lurch, she was not sure where. She tried to narrow her thoughts down, focus on the fact she needed to solve this mystery. To keep the idea that she was talking to a real live ghost – a real *dead* ghost – away from the front of her mind.

'He is, isn't he? I can, well… I can tell.'

The woman opened her mouth in a despondent sigh that Alice heard. Later, she would be sure that she had imagined it, because the ghost at all times remained silent.

The woman had stopped rocking, although she remained in the poised, panther-like position. Watching her.

Alice took a step closer. She lifted her hand towards the woman.

'I want to do everything I can for you,' she said. 'I'm not scared. I've seen ghosts before. I know you don't mean any harm.'

She took another step forward.

'I'm going to take a wild guess about the boy in the hood – is he your son?'

The room which was cold anyway seemed to plunge in temperature. The woman wrinkled her nose, very hard, anguish in her dark eyes. She clamped her teeth together.

Alice thought about the pump in the feeder pipe, the boy's grey foot – or exposed sock, surely?

'Did he – did he drown… in the lake?'

For a moment, Alice had never felt so close to any creature before. Tears began to stream from the corners of her eyes. She remembered a funeral, when she was a girl, of one of her dad's school friends who had died young, of cystic fibrosis. It took place in a small, beautiful whitewashed chapel and they were – on the bequest of the family of course – playing mellow indie music which made her feel emotional even though she scarcely knew the man. She could see a woman further down the pew, a young woman in black with a netted hat, dabbing her face with a handkerchief. And then they changed the music to a beautiful, fast, mystical pop song, *Sometimes* by James, and suddenly she could feel it in the air, everyone wanted to wail and cry until the day they died for this terrible situation they all found themselves in. How could it be like this, so beautiful and so unbearable? It was too much, it was not possible.

With the ghost's pain in front of her, Alice felt like she had at that funeral. She remembered that mass feeling of grief and ridiculous, exquisite suffering. Except this time, the feeling was coming from one being, one dead being, instead of many living ones.

'How…' She sobbed, deeply, and stopped. Looked at the ghost. Held the ghost's startling brown eyes.

165

'How did it happen?'

The woman jerked her head upwards. The second time, Alice realised she was beckoning for her to come over to her.

Alice nodded her understanding.

The red-rimmed eyes stared wildly at her. Alice could feel the power, the intense concentration to do – to do what?

Contain her sanity.

Alice walked forward and kept her eyes wide open as she pressed her face into the wild woman's own...

## 68

*She is running, running again, fast across the sunlit lawn, a shadowy figure, a man, shouting, behind her.*

*'Mary – Mary, slow down!'*

*But she won't slow down, how can she, she had seen him splashing in the water, in the lake, still in that coat he wore despite the weather, seen him disappear from sight...*

*What had he been doing?*

*Climbing that tree, the big one, she could see now, see the jagged branch that was broken, half in, half out of the lake.*

*The lake with its still water, blinking with sunlight.*

*The lake with its hunched, facedown, floating boy.*

*The boy in the burgundy hood.*

*Her boy.*

*Seeing there, just under the water, a flash of grey, one of his socks, his pump missing...*

*She remembers her words, like nails in her brain.*

*'Go on, off with you, Petey. Play in the garden. Me and Jerry don't wanna see you around for the next hour.'*

Afterwards, as she pulled back from the shock, from the guilt and horror, Alice would realize that *stopped* was too ineffectual a word for what the ghost did then. She dipped her head, ceased all her rocking, and let her hair hang down to the blanket on top of the bed.

Loading. That's what she was doing. She was centring herself, honing down to the core of her pain. Loading herself for what came next. Everything went into suspension – except for the blood, thick and brutal in Alice's veins.

When the ghost finally moved, it was in a massive blur. Much of it Alice had to reconstruct in her mind's eye afterwards. The woman jerked upright, a hand coming to the neck of her shabby dress and yanking it down, exposing a wound at the top of her breast, similar to the one she had shown on her hand. Alice noticed what seemed like marks, puffy like a bee or wasp sting, a streak of red trailing down from one.

She scarcely took it in before the woman had three-quarters reversed herself on the bed and was staring defiantly over her shoulder at Alice as she showed a rip in the back of her dress and – ugh – a much larger, open wound, black blood all around torn flesh. Alice jerked her head back in pain and disgust.

Then the ghost sprang up from the bed and ran away, straight through the wall.

There was no way she was following. Not this time.

Alice stumbled forward and collapsed face down on the bed. She let out a great wailing sob, muffled by the blanket. For a while her head was overloaded with emotion, a blind rush into nothing but torture and sorrow. She felt like a tiny minnow, swimming in an ocean of chaos and destruction.

And it had all come from the woman.

Her *pain*.

What had happened to her? She wished so much that the woman could talk. But at least this time she had found out more, through her memories and the strength of her feeling. Her emotion had taken over the whole room.

The boy in the burgundy hood was her son. She knew that now, she was sure of it.

And he had died – drowned – in the feeder lake, while his mum, Mary, was – was what? Cavorting around the house with… who? Jerry?

Tears flooded her eyes as she sensed the great anguish, the harrowed guilt of the ghost again.

Ghosts hang around. They hang around because of something terrible, tragic, something unbearable that happened in their lives. Or they hang around because they need to convey something to someone. Like the reading man who let her know ghosts could help, or Charlotte's gran who came to protect her granddaughter. Or her own mum, who found the medium of her phone to warn her of this coming horror…

The dreadful injuries the woman had showed her were clearly a major part of her story. But nevertheless,

Alice couldn't help but feel that the reason Mary was here – still here in Bramley – was not to do with the wounds. It was because of her guilt. Her soul-destroying guilt.

She had neglected her son, left him alone in an unfamiliar place.

And she had paid a terrible price.

### 71

Now she knew how the boy had died. But what had happened to his mother, Mary? Was the man Jerry anything to do with it?

Alice needed to speak to Fran. She had to escalate this now.

And… was she really going to spend the rest of the night here in Bramley – alone?

The thought made her feel queasy. She sat up on the bed. Whilst she definitely did *not* fancy the idea of going downstairs she knew that she needed tea, hot sweet tea to restore the sugar in her blood, to stop herself from shaking. Her mind - and her vision – were literally shaking! Whilst she'd never been trained, she knew enough about First Aid to realise she was suffering from shock.

She concentrated for the next few moments on steadying her breathing. For a while she worried that it wouldn't ever slow down, that her heart would pound against her ribcage until it was nothing but a broken pulp.

This was ridiculous. What had she got herself into?

Thankfully, after a while, her heartbeat slowed to a steady thump, not normal, but nothing to inspire panic.

She stood up and, determinedly putting the fear out of her mind, left the room and went down to the kitchen.

As she stood beside the boiling kettle she tried not to glance at the dark windows for fear they would freak her out again. Her imagination was showing her all kinds of spectres leering back in at her. She remembered a time when her mum had put her to bed in their old house and she had been frightened by a programme they'd watched, just a regular American cop series, but this episode had featured a serial killer who wore a Mickey Mouse mask and crept up on his victims to stab them from behind. Alice was worried that someone would come into their house. Don't worry, her mum had told her, if anyone comes Bless (their intelligent, four-year-old Schnauzer) will bark. And at that moment, from the downstairs hall, Bless had let out the most almighty yowl. It scared her mum as much as it scared her. They both ran downstairs, only to find the dog standing alert but with no one and nothing there.

Stop thinking frightening thoughts, Alice told herself now.

She knew that with fear, ninety-nine percent of the damage was done by yourself.

She had to keep her mind empty. Everything would feel different in the morning. Very different.

Still, she jumped half out of her skin when the kettle clacked off beside her. Then she made her tea, showered it with sugar from the bowl, and headed back upstairs.

## 72

Before she woke fully the next morning, she flittered and blinked between dream and consciousness. Again, she was within the cramped, burdened space of the ghost woman's feelings, struggling to move this way and that to get out, to break free, to leave *him*, the man who had caused all this, behind. And to free herself from the unbearable loss of her son, to somehow make amends.

She felt her chest constrict and gave a sharp gasp as she came awake fully.

After a moment she realised what she had to do.

Whilst they were both in the same house, she had never seen the woman and her son together.

She knew – *knew* – that to help the ghost, to help poor Mary, she had somehow to reunite her with her son.

But how?

73

Alice drew back the curtains to see the stark, ice-encrusted snowscape of the Bramley gardens. After dressing, she opened her window and looked down to see that the moat was entirely frozen over, pale whorls of ice across the darkness below. She shut it quickly and went downstairs.

Without any easy answers as to how she might bring Mary back to her son, Alice decided to get out to the stumpery again, to investigate the concealed structure for any further signs that it might be an underground Roman temple. But first she forced herself to make some porridge and drink some tea.

As she sat eating beside the warm Aga, she considered what she had learnt before her harrowing encounter with Mary, from reading Forbes' books about the Mithras cult.

First things first. It wasn't called a Mystery Religion for nothing. Almost everything that archaeologists and historians thought about Mithraism was conjecture. The evidence was scant, principally the numerous temples themselves with their pictures of Mithras undertaking the killing of the bull with his animal companions, the snake, scorpion and dog. Historians speculated that this sacrifice, like that of Jesus (who shared his birthday with Mithras) enabled salvation of the faithful. The ceremony was often watched over by Aion, or Chronos, the lion-headed man who was associated in some way with time and the changing of the seasons. In essence, the Mithras cult was thought to be a guild for working- and middle-class men of the Empire, especially soldiers and tradesmen. It afforded initiates protection against the vagaries of an unpredictable world, and its seven rites of passage were believed to have inspired modern-day Masonry.

That much was all straightforward. What was interesting about reading Forbes' second book, was how much he picked over the various theories of his day on the cult, and how much he read into them. Time and again as she was reading Alice wondered whether Forbes believed it all himself.

She finished her porridge and checked the time. 8.35. Early. But she was so hyped up by the temple and the ghost that she had to try Fran.

She made the call but there was no answer. She was going to leave a message but decided against it. She had to hear Fran's reaction when she told her there was – almost certainly – a Roman temple in the grounds. On reflection, she realised she needed to wait until they were face to face before talking to her about Mary and the boy in the hood.

She swigged the last of her tea, cleared up, looked out the window at the beautiful snow on the lawn.

She tried the number again. Still no answer. This time she left a message, but just telling Fran to call her back.

The urgency was killing her. Maybe she could get Fran in her office? The RM hadn't given her any other number besides her mobile, but she could try anyway. She had to go upstairs, right round to the chapel, to find enough signal to do a web search. She found the page for regional contacts but annoyingly there was only a postal and email address for their area.

Her impatience was killing her. She rang the main switchboard number.

'Trust for England, how can I help you today?' said a woman, in a broad Geordie accent.

'Hi, yes, I'm Alice Deaton, the manager at your new Bramley property. I'm trying to get through to Fran McDowd in the regional team. Can you connect me?'

'Shouldn't be a problem, let me just check.'

There was a pause.

'McDowell, did you say? M-C-D-O-W-E-double-L?'

'No, McDowd, with a d on the end.'

'McDowd. OK, I've got you… No, I can't seem to find her on the list.'

'Oh.'

'It's not unusual, sorry to say. The list is notoriously out of date. When did she start?'

'I don't know. A long time ago, I think.'

'The last person someone wanted to speak to was the Chief Finance Officer. Even *she* wasn't on the list! Do you want me to put you through to the main number for the regional office?'

'Yes please.'

After a few rings the phone in the regional office went to the answer machine. Evidently still too early for the regional folk.

'Hello, this is Alice Deaton at Bramley, leaving a message for Fran. Can she call me back on my mobile, 079655550 please? It's urgent. Thanks.'

Why did she say the number? Fran would have it in her phone.

Still. *Still.*

She put on her scarf and coat and headed out through the snow to the stumpery.

<br>

74

<br>

In the snow-buried dell behind the stumpery, Alice stood looking at the partially exposed door.

It clearly hadn't been used for years, possibly even centuries. She wondered whether Forbes himself might be the last one to have used it.

It was odd, she thought, to see it buried like that. If Forbes had discovered such a precious archaeological site, surely he would have made it into a feature at Bramley? Why would he – or perhaps subsequent owners – have covered it up again?

She supposed it might have been done to preserve it. That was quite a common archaeological practice. Dig it out, do all the learning, photography, and cataloguing and then bury it again to save it from weather and the trample of unknowing folk. But then, from what he'd written Forbes appeared so keen, almost an adherent of Mithras. She could imagine him in his passion – his zealotry, as it sometimes seemed – performing obscure astrological rituals here.

So why re-bury it? Unless…

She looked up at the snowy shoulders of the dell above her, the jutting sandstone slabs, interlaced with the muscular, pythonic roots of mature hollies. She had approached the dell from the stumpery on the eastern edge. She hadn't yet explored the other side, the western side.

The snow was deep in the dell, so it took some effort to scramble up the bank to the right of the portal. Towards the top it became steeper and she had to reach up and grab for one of the stone lips, then haul herself up. She put a knee into the snow to stop herself toppling backwards into the dell.

With a gasp, she was on the top, on the other flank of the prickly thicket.

She headed along the bank of hollies, some hefty sycamores covered in furry moss on her other side. There were clumps of hart's tongue fern ahead, before the holly swept back into her path, obscuring the view of the stumpery below.

She didn't notice the sudden drop until she was almost upon it. It was hidden by a huge beech tree with raised, knotted roots all around it. Only as she began to clamber over the tangled roots did she stop, seeing the drop just beyond. The tree was anchored precariously to the bank, its giant tap root exposed.

She gasped as she looked down into the concealed dip.

'God, is that another door?' she muttered.

In her excitement at getting to it she managed to jar her knee sliding down the bank. But even the jab of pain couldn't stop her springing up and rushing into this other concealed opening in the holly-covered knoll.

Shaking off snow and earth, she came to a halt in front of a second door. This one was tall and thin, made out of wood, black with age. It had four panels and a small, tarnished bronze doorknob. Alice thought that if it weren't for the weathering, the door wouldn't look out of place inside the house. Well, the weathering and the fact there was a wooden bar across it, held in place by two rusty iron brackets.

She lifted the bar and set it down on the ground, then turned the handle and pushed.

The door scraped across stone as it opened.

Alice walked tentatively into the darkness beyond.

75

Except as soon as she was inside the damp, cave-like space, she realised that it was not, in fact, completely dark. Up ahead there was a small patch of silvery-grey light, a patch of daylight, illuminating a section of floor and a pair of heavy-set brick pillars.

Alice realised that it must be coming from the sliver of the trench above the stumpery. The trench dug out by George…

The patch of daylight was not enough for her to properly explore, so she fished her phone out of her pocket and shook on the torch. She found she was in a long, narrow chamber with pillars on either side. The ceiling, a few feet overhead, was vaulted like a wine cellar. The floor was laid with uneven grey flagstones. In the torchlight she could see perhaps fifteen foot ahead. Three sets of pillars flanked the central walkway. She could not make out the section of the room between where her torchlight faded and the daylight broke through. Nor could she tell how much further the room continued.

Alice breathed in. The room smelt of old, damp, stale earth. With a hint of something else. Oil? A burnt wick?

She felt her chest tightening, like an allergic reaction. She coughed, and walked forwards.

Ahead, a long, stone table with benches on either side came into sight. Strangely, plates, cutlery and glasses had been set on the table. There were two black candleholders filled with burned-down candles. She went and leaned close to them, realising this was where the other smell came from. These plates, the cutlery – it looked like they were from the house. The table had been laid for dinner…

She shone her torch around the backs of the pillars, seeing bare brick walls just beyond them on one side and, on the other, what must surely be the sealed-up door into the dell. She noticed how small and thin the bricks were, compared to today's standards. She shifted the torch beam up again, and continued down the room.

She reached the section beneath the opening in the ceiling. A little snow – as well as a few bits of rubble – had fallen through and settled on the floor. She kicked the rubble away and looked up.

The gap that George had dug was thin enough to have covered over with snow, like a scar healing with translucent skin. Holding her phone above her head she could see that the hole in the ceiling had not been broken out. The bricks ended neatly there, although looking closely she could see that there were a few frayed edges where some of them had broken. Leading away from one edge was a fairly significant crack, zigzagging its way through the mortar. But the vent was clearly part of the design.

She recalled something from Forbes' books, something about the tauroctony, the slaying of the bull. A few of the Mithras temples had been discovered with openings like this and some historians believed they were vents at which bulls had been sacrificed, allowing the blood to soak the initiates below.

Gruesome.

For a moment, a slightly panicked moment, she thought about the red bull in the upper field. Tom Gauge's bull.

She turned and shone her light forwards down the chamber. At once, the most splendid statues appeared, set within a deep alcove in the far wall. She recognised them, and walked towards what she now knew, had she ever doubted, was truly a shrine to the Roman god Mithras.

'Oh, my giddy aunt...' she muttered, stepping around a small stone altar to examine them.

She had seen several depictions of the god now, but this one differed in that Mithras himself was almost the same size as the bull. With one hand reaching towards Alice with a dagger, he pulled the bull's head up by its jaw, exposing its throat. As he did so the bull was set upon by a viper, a dog, and – yes, there, at the bottom, as she expected – a scorpion, striking its testicles with its stinger.

'You poor, poor beast,' she said.

Behind him, on a plinth in the wall, the sun god Sol looked on. To either side, two lion-headed men stood sentinel with long staves. And… what were those?

She shone the torch down and saw that there were two boxes in the corner behind the statue, a smaller perched on top of a larger one. No, not boxes – glass tanks, like aquariums. Except without water.

She knelt down to take a closer look.

'Oh – my – God…' She felt her skin shrink around her skull.

The tanks were not empty.

Seized by a sudden fear, Alice turned and hurried out of the underground chamber.

76

She half-ran, half-jumped down the snow-laden bank and forced her way into the line of holly trees. Ignoring scratches, she broke out into the disturbing landscape of the stumpery.

And stopped, her breath fogging the air, her head and neck clammy with sweat.

What was going on? What were they doing?

The cap on the armchair in the Solar room – it was a Phrygian cap. When she got back from the Lakes the night before last and saw them dressed in those long coats – had they been down here? Maybe in robes? The person with them, with the dark hair – was it George?

179

And now this, the confirmation that it was a Temple of Mithras. But, most disconcertingly, to find that someone was keeping a live snake and a scorpion down there!

She felt competing pressures in her brain, as if it were being shoved and probed by amorphous tentacles. Everything around, as she made her way through the snow-layered stumpery, was quiet, still, in contrast to the turmoil inside her.

Was this real?

Was it possible – could they be – were they planning perhaps… *to kill a bull?*

Her processing of reality was such a struggle that it took her a moment to realise what the throbbing in her pocket was. And then the sound, the electronic drum intro to *Sound and Vision*.

Her phone. It was ringing.

She drew it out, saw an unknown number, a landline.

She pressed the green button.

'Hello, can I speak to… Alice Deaton, please?' said a man's voice.

'It's me.'

'Hi, my name is Richard Croft. I'm calling from the Trust for England regional office. You left a message on our answerphone. Said it was urgent.'

'Er – yes. God, it's you. Um, yes, right. So, yes, I need to update Fran on some things that have happened at Bramley. They're urgent. Is she there?'

'Fran? Yes, I heard that on the message. Are you sure it's Fran?'

'Yes, Fran. The Regional Manager.'

'So – I'm the Regional Manager. It's me. Richard Croft.'

'But Fran… Fran McDowd told me it was her.'

The man laughed, nervously. 'I'm not sure who you mean. There's no Fran here.'

Alice thought of an adze, one of those broad-bladed axe-like tools for cutting wood. She thought of one cleaving her insides.

'She's a – a large woman. She's been overseeing my work here at Bramley.'

'Bramley?'

'Yes. Bramley.'

Again – nervously – the man laughed. 'I'm guessing you mean the moated house near Loveton?'

Alice felt a sprig of relief. 'Yes, of course. The one taken on a year or so ago. I'm the new manager. Fran has been supervising me…'

'Taken on – by who?'

'By us… by the Trust for England, of course.'

There was an icy pause. A tiny bird, a wren, swooped low through the dead yews in front of her, vanishing into the scrub.

'I think we've got some wires crossed here,' said Richard at last.

'What do you mean?'

'I do know the property you're talking about. Beautiful place, owned by an old couple.'

'Yes!'

'They approached us years ago. Before my time. But I remember reading through the paperwork. It's still on the development long list. Think we even drew up some Heads of Terms…'

'Yes – yes…'

'But they never signed them. I believe…' he stretched out the word *believe*, '… that they were on the verge of signing when they had some kind of major turnaround in their finances. An investment on the stock market came off. Or something.'

She couldn't find the words.

'Are you still there?'

No one is here, she thought. I have to get out *now*.

She slipped the phone into her pocket, without even thinking to end the call. She ran down through the stumpery, out into the orchard, the straggly black branches of the fruit trees all lined with snow. Beyond, below, Bramley with its brown timbers sitting strong and grey in its frozen moat. She ran through the Kitchen garden, the burial – *vegetable* – plots covered in humps of snow. She ran down the side of the great lawn, alongside the house, across the bridge – throwing a glance towards her snow-covered car – and through the gate. She ran past the laurel planters, across the cobbles, opened the door into the entrance hall. She ran through the Great Hall, past the witch wards on the fireplace, the portrait of Forbes, through the corridor to the Library, thinking, I should have talked to him, I should have discussed what has happened and got him to send someone over – or perhaps even call the police – but now all she had to do was get her keys and get out, there was no one here, the S-Js had gone away, she had plenty of time but she didn't care about that, she just needed to get out first and sort out this – this what? – this freak show of ideas in her head, she would drive out to town, maybe even further, to Telford or somewhere, a big town or city where she would more definitely be safe, somewhere away from this unbelievable place…

At the top of the stairs she shuddered, passing the door to the S-J's apartments. Who were these people? Or

182

perhaps it was just George – she couldn't think, don't think about it now, she ran on down the corridor, found her key and with shaking fingers opened her door.

The car keys were on the small table in front of the fire. Quickly, she shoved a few of her things into her backpack, then ran back out through the open door on to the landing. She closed the door behind her then looked down the corridor – and froze.

George was standing at the end of the landing.

He was wearing his old green Barbour. At a distance, his wavy hair was like a shaggy Afro.

He was looking at her, standing still.

'George,' she said, forcing a smile.

He started to walk towards her.

'There you are,' she said.

He smiled and began making hand gestures as he approached, pointing to her backpack, mouthing something that she was sure meant, *where are you going?*

She wondered whether she should run.

She watched him wide-eyed as he drew nearer.

'I've been looking for you,' she said, hearing her voice quaver. She couldn't think of anything else that might sound even vaguely normal.

'And now you've found me,' he said.

77

His voice was quite high but with a cultivated edge to it.

'You spoke,' she whispered.

'God be praised, it's a miracle!' he said, his face breaking into a broad smile, showing his yellowed, slightly crooked teeth.

183

Alice swung her pack off her shoulder and straight at his head. He managed to duck a little, put an arm up to reduce the full force of the blow, but it still bounced against the side of his face.

She turned and ran.

She ran along the latticed windows to the galleried staircase, the one the boy in the burgundy hood had used. George was right behind her, hammering along the corridor.

She leapt down the stairs, swinging herself through a hundred-and-eighty degrees around the bannister at the bottom, seeing him framed by the giant window in the quarter-landing, only feet away from her. She hurtled into the crypt, past the kitchen, slamming the library door behind her to give herself a few paces extra lead before he rattled the handle, threw it open.

'Stop!' he shouted.

Out of the Library, out of the Great Hall, out of the entrance lobby, across the cobblestones, she knew she had just one chance.

The gate. She glanced behind as she entered the covered walkway, he was in the middle of the courtyard, running like a madman.

If it hadn't been open she wouldn't have had a hope.

But it was. She ran out, turned and shoved it closed with her shoulder. The key was out of her pocket in her hand and in the lock, turning swiftly even as she heard the hefty latch being lifted on the other side.

The ancient gate held. Designed to keep people out, it now kept one in.

Her whole body shook as she ran across the bridge, snow crunching underfoot, and over to her car. As she fumbled for her keys she realised with another shot of panic that she couldn't feel with her fingertips, her fingers were so cold. She tugged all of the keys in her pocket, watched them fall into the snow in a splay of iron like a dark star exploding.

She stooped down and curled her pink fingers around the set with the car key, lifting them up, feeling a numbness in her wrist as she forced her thumb and forefinger to grasp the right key, slide it after several scratching attempts into the door.

When she opened the car door she heard a crashing sound behind her. Startled, she looked over her shoulder and saw that one of the windows in the house was open, one of those in the Squire's room. She imagined she would see George peering out at her, shouting to her – but he wasn't there.

The windscreen was thick with snow. Something bad was happening to her muscles, the cold and fear were starting to mess with them. But still, the snow had to be cleared and her arm was the best tool for the job. She swept the crust away, leaving thin streaks of ice still showing. But at least she would be able to see.

She climbed into the driver seat. Before going through the shenanigans of trying to make her fingers do what she needed them to do and get the *bloody key in the ignition*, she turned to lock the door.

And gasped.

George was clambering over the top of the moat wall, his black hair plastered around his bright pink face, his clothes drenched through.

He had jumped into the moat! The crash was his body breaking through the ice. He must have climbed out using Forbes' old ladder for swimming.

She pushed the key at the ignition, her face contorted in a grimace. Her bloody hands wouldn't work!

'Come on!' she shouted. Then louder: 'Come on!'

The key locked in. A quick glance showed George halfway across the drive, closing on her. He looked crazy, absolutely demented.

She brought up her left hand to help twist her right wrist. The force wasn't enough, the car engine churned once and then nothing. She tried again, even slower this time, there was no sound from the bonnet at all.

'Shit…' she said, unable to resist a glance to her right.

George had bent down to pick something up off the ground – one of the smooth round stones used to delineate the edge of the parking area, the size of a bloomer.

'Shit,' she gasped, as with another desperate twist the engine kicked into life. She slammed it into reverse, craned her neck and swung the car around in a semi-circle to face the driveway. She heard the muffled sound of tyres pulverising fresh snow. She looked up and saw George almost upon her, soaked through, lifting the heavy stone up above his shoulders.

She floored the accelerator, the car didn't stall, she spun forward.

There was a sound like an explosion and white and silver showered around her like a waterfall. The car wobbled and stopped. The stone was on the seat beside her and there was blood on her knuckles, wrapped around the steering wheel.

The car had stalled. The windscreen was, on her side, a mass of white frost, on the passenger side, a gaping hole through which, somehow, George managed to thrust a fist and strike her on the side of the head.

Her neck jarred and the back of her skull bounced on the headrest. She felt a fuzziness in her head, accompanied by numbness in her body. She was able to watch incomprehensively as he leaned in, and hit her again.

Her world went.

*In the Dark*

78

Juddering.

She became aware of the jerky movement first, before she opened her eyes, certainly before she thought. Her arms and legs were rocking randomly, splayed about her. Her face was turned sideways. Her neck was stiff. When she did open her eyes she was looking at a bird table on a lawn covered in a thick icing of snow. The bird table was shuddering away, disappearing from her field of vision.

The memory of what happened was ice too, a chilling strike into the heart that made her sit bolt upright – or try to. She was strapped on a table, no, on a trailer, the strap pulled tight across her chest. Looking upwards, tilting her neck, she saw the back of the lawn mower, the back of the man driving it.

George, now wearing a woolly hat over his black mop.

She tried again to get up, twisting desperately as the mower swung sharply to the left and began to ascend an incline around the far wall of the Kitchen garden. She knew at once where he was taking her.

She had to escape!

Her jaw was sore and her head ached. The strap was pinning her torso down, but her arms could move a little. If she pushed herself down, she was able to bend her elbows. Her fingers came up to the buckle which was right across her heart. But once again, their power to move was sapped by the bitter cold. She could barely feel her fingertips, let alone generate enough leverage to counter the tension of the strap and lift the clip.

Still, she tried.

But pretty soon the tone of the mower's engine dropped. The trailer began to slow. She knew they had arrived at the stumpery.

Alice forced herself to relax her limbs.

She shut her eyes.

### 79

She felt one of his hands brush across her forehead and eyebrows and come down on her left breast. It took all her will not to jerk up in a spasm of fear and revulsion.

Thankfully, he was only holding her down as a counterpoint to releasing the ratcheted strap, which he did swiftly with the other hand. The pressure on her chest dropped. Behind her eyelids her eyes darted wildly about in panic as he lifted her up under her arms and then hauled her over his shoulder.

George trudged through the snow, carrying her up the hill. She felt him weave about and opened her eyes fleetingly to see the rotted stumps passing by.

'Do you know why I know you're awake?'

Alice fought to remain calm, to stop her body tensing. She shut her eyes.

'It's no use pretending.'

She held her breath, tried to flop with the movement of his steps. They couldn't be far away from the holly bank now.

'When you're unconscious your eyes don't move at all if they're touched. I tried that one out on Mary, too. But she *was* unconscious.'

A terror exploded inside her then but she scarcely had time to register it as suddenly she was swung off his shoulder and down into the snow. Instinctively she reacted to prevent herself landing hard on her back. When the blur of movement was over she found herself sitting on her backside, legs apart, staring up at him.

She wasn't sure how she did it but next she was up and on her feet trying to run back into the stumpery but immediately he had her around the waist, both of them crashing down on to the ground.

'No you don't!'

'Let go of me!'

As he pushed himself up on top of her she tried to kick him, to knee him between the legs, but he was too strong.

'Shall I hit you again?'

She ceased struggling. Reluctantly, she stared up into his face, suspended above hers, frosted breath escaping from his lips. He reeked of garlic. She felt sick.

'No,' she said.

'Good,' he said, baring his teeth. Was he mad?

As he eased off her and pulled her up she summoned all her courage and asked:

'What are you doing, George?'

'It's Jerry,' he said.

'God,' she whispered, as he took her wrist and began leading her towards the holly.

'It worked last time, it'll work again,' he said.

'What?' she said.

'I like to call it – and I can call it what I like, seeing as it was my idea – Tauroctony Plus.'

'Mithras. You worship that old Roman god, don't you? You're going to kill a bull. The one in the upper field?'

He stopped and looked at her brightly. 'You clever girl, you've worked out a lot, haven't you?' He looked genuinely impressed.

'Why – why all this? What will it achieve?'

'Well, on the evidence of last time, quite a lot. These old mystery gods, there's not a lot of people paying them homage anymore, as you can imagine. Just a few Illuminati and small covens dotted around. So they are extremely grateful when anyone does take them seriously. And they *will* reward them.'

'When was the last time?'

'Nine years ago.'

'When the Smythe-Johnstones first approached the Trust to help them out…'

'You really are doing well,' said the man – said Jerry. He began to pull her away again, thrusting her with him into the shrubbery. Alice felt the holly scratching at her hands and face, but then they were through to the other side and she could see the giant, precarious beech tree – and the wooden door. Everything was oddly hushed by the snow, like a theatre just before the performance begins.

'Why on earth did you pretend to be deaf and dumb? And your name…' Alice knew she had to find out as

191

much as she could in this moment, whilst he was being so talkative. She had a feeling that he was going to lock her in the temple and the more sense she could make of her situation, the better she felt her chance of... what?

Of survival.

'One's got to make one's own fun,' he said. The look he gave her, all bright eyed and bushy-tailed, as her dad would have said, made her think he *was* mad.

'So you killed a bull nine years ago – wearing your Phrygian outfit, no doubt,' she added, realising that it *was* him she'd seen two nights ago with the S-Js, of course it was. 'And then there was a turnaround in the S-J's finances – some investment came off, they didn't need to compromise with the Trust – and you thought the two were connected.'

He laughed. 'Priceless!' he said. 'You're so nearly there!'

'What else?'

'The killing of the bull brought in a little funding. But it was Mary who turned our fortunes round.'

Shit.

She felt like there was no air in her chest, nothing to talk with. But still, she tried.

'Who – who was Mary?'

'My girlfriend.'

Alice thought of the Instagram account, the pretty girl with the gap in her teeth, laughing in the garden. The ghost of Bramley.

'You killed your girlfriend?'

'Yes.'

'God...'

'She was one of those very rare characters who live under the radar. A shocking childhood. Abused by her father *and* mother, living in temporary accommodation all the time, moving from one rotten estate to another, all over the Midlands and Wales. Never in the same place for long, never claiming benefits, never working for anything except cash in hand. Occasional prostitution, money from pimps and abusive partners, I'm sure you've heard of the type. It took a long time to find her. A long time to find the right person.'

She was reminded of a shocking TV documentary she'd seen on the Gloucestershire serial killers, Rosemary and Fred West, the way they had killed women that the authorities hardly knew existed. No one to know they'd gone missing, tortured to death and buried beneath the West's cellar and garden patio.

Breathe. *Breathe…*

'And now, through a far more ingenious process, we've found the right one again,' said Jerry. 'The ideal candidate, you might say!'

## 80

'Did you have a son?' said Alice, as she was tugged towards the door. She fought back a desire to cry, she could feel the wetness in her eyes. 'You and Mary?'

'The boy in the hood? You've seen him too?'

'Yes.'

'No, not me and her. The boy was hers from a previous boyfriend – or client.'

'And he died…'

'Yes. Died here. In an accident. His mother and I were having some fun inside when poor little Petey decided to climb a tree, out over the lake. The branch broke and he drowned. She never did get over it. Not that she suffered for long. We killed her soon after.'

'Monster…'

'What's that?'

Alice looked up. 'Do you see them too, then? The ghosts?'

'No. Poor old Dad's the only one who sees them. That's why he has to get out sometimes. It gets too much for him. Why he went last night.'

He stopped at the door and smiled. 'The look on your face,' he said.

Alice felt as if her life had drained out of her. She felt dead, almost.

'You didn't realise I was their son?' said Jerry. 'No reason you should, I suppose. But I just thought, with you having worked out so much by now, you might have got it. Do you really think I'd do all this out of loyalty to my employers?' He chuckled. 'No, I really don't plan to lose my inheritance, what's rightfully mine – and my sister's.'

He swung the door open and shoved her forwards.

Alice shrieked as he stepped back, grinning, and slammed it shut.

She heard him pull down the bar and jam it firmly into place.

## 81

Of course, he had taken her phone.

Alice walked down the dark temple, feeling ahead to make sure she didn't bash into the table. When she found it she shuffled around it until she reached the end nearest

194

the patch of daylight from the overhead incision. Then she sat on the edge of the table and bellowed:

'No!'

'No!' And again: 'No!'

She ended up choking on tears, struggling to bring in breath against her paralysed diaphragm.

'No…'

She left herself, left all thought and reason behind, consumed by loss, grief and an abysmal terror.

## 82

She might have been there like that for hours or it could have been a few minutes.

Her mind had to travel a vast, inconceivable space just to return to itself.

Eventually, thoughts and feelings began to feel referenced again.

Someone was glimpsing them, trying to catch them. Trying to catch the rain.

Someone. Her. Alice.

How could this be?

How?

## 83

There was self-reproach, verging on self-loathing.

How could she ever have thought the Trust for England would appoint her, Alice, a quiet deputy manager in a nowhere community centre, to develop and open one of its most promising new properties? A medieval bloody manor in the middle of beautiful bloody countryside?

How could she ever have been so stupid?

There would have been hundreds of highly qualified applicants for a post like that. With a frighteningly perverse sense of satisfaction and discovery, she tried to work out their thinking.

Put an ad in just a few small local papers, in places where the Trust didn't have properties and was unlikely to have any actual staff see it. Copy the logo. Instead of using the online application process (why didn't that trigger it for her?), ask for a CV and accompanying letter – sent to an email address that was clearly made up – it had trustforengland in it but wasn't it .net or something obvious, not .org? Ask a pointed question about self-sufficiency, being away from friends and families for long periods.

And then the interview. Just a one-to-one with Fran – whoever she really is – and then the second meeting with the S-Js. All those unimportant, poorly thought-through questions about property management – she chuckled, black humour, thinking how pleased she'd been, how lucky she'd felt at how simple they had seemed – and then followed by all the questions on family, friends and relationships, especially from Bernard and Samantha.

All the time looking, searching for the right candidate. The one whose parents were both dead, who didn't have siblings or a husband or a boyfriend (at least at the time). The introvert with no close friends to speak of.

How many had they rejected?

How could they have been so brazen? So desperate?

And how could *she* ever have been so stupid?

## 84

For a while she lost herself to tremendous, wretched self-pity, sprawled across the table, head in hands, sobbing quietly.

Then she began to notice the cold, to feel the numb seeping through her limbs, saturating the core of her.

She could die of hypothermia down here.

The shock of the idea brought to mind the even more chilling idea – the truly petrifying idea – of what they planned to do to her.

They were going to kill her! To sacrifice her to a long-forgotten Roman deity. She thought about the tapestry she'd cleaned, obviously stained with blood from the first 'sacrifice'. And she thought about the snake and the scorpion, just a few feet away in the dark alcove. Waiting silently, unknowing, for the perverse roles lined up for them.

Alice thought about Mary, Mary's ghost, on all fours on her bed, displaying her raw wounds. The puncture mark on the hand, the two bleeding pinpricks on her chest, the torn flesh of her back. The scorpion, the snake, the dog. The dog? Oh my god. Henry, of course. How could they make a dog do that? She remembered something someone had once told her, a drunken conversation in a bar, about how dogs would eat their owners without hesitation if they died at home and the dog got hungry. Maybe they'd starved poor Henry for a day.

And all with the insane delusion that such an act would turn around their fortunes. Give them another decade without having to divest ownership of their precious home. Which was so much more to them than mere bricks and mortar. It was their culture, their identity, their very lives. What was it Bernard had said? In some way, for them, it was England itself…

No doubt about it, she was dealing with a family that was insane.

Or rather, given the hopelessness of her situation, *they* were dealing with her.

Alice wanted to panic. She trembled, remembering her teenage anxiety. If that were to return now, she would be lost. A gibbering wreck for the S-Js to carve up as they would.

She had to focus.

Remember who she was.

She had to… to what?

She had to get angry.


## 85

It was all in the mind now.

How dare they do this to her?

These people actually thought they could mess around with her life, play on her ambitions, remove her from her home, all to this sick end. But… why had they taken so long to do it? Surely once she was here they could have just welcomed her in, bashed her on the head with a spade and got on with it?

She thought about her predecessor, the girl they 'hadn't got on with'. Alice knew now why that was. She would have appeared just as virginal (not the right word, but it conveyed the right sentiment) as her, but then, when she took the job and moved in, they must have discovered some connection about her, some intimate friend or unrevealed family member that meant her life was being witnessed from afar. Someone who surprised them, just like Matthew had done.

*That* was why they hadn't killed Alice at once. She shook her head as the full weight of the revelation dawned on her. It was all down to Matthew, the boyfriend she had found in between the interview and starting the job. She imagined their fear, their worry about having to sack another one – only for the situation to resolve itself when she and Matthew broke up, almost as quickly as they had come together.

All crystal clear now, she thought. All clear now.


## 86

How dare they?

She stood up.

She had to get out of this place.

Before she froze to death. Before they came back to butcher her.

She looked up at the long slit in the roof above her. More snow had fallen – *snow on snow*, she thought – and the open patch had turned from white to grey. In places the gap was about six inches wide, nowhere near big enough to squeeze through.

How stable was the roof? she wondered. Could she break some of those bricks to make enough room for her to get through?

She looked around for something to stand on. The table and benches were stone, far too heavy to move. Likewise the statue of Mithras, whose hand and dagger she could just make out in the darkness. What about the tanks with the snake and the scorpion?

The gloom seemed to lift a little as she ventured into it, away from the daylight. She could make out the rest of the statue, the deeper, disorientating blackness of the alcove beyond. She reached down and felt the edge of the smaller glass tank, the one with the scorpion. She picked it up and carried it back into the half-light, noticing that the bottom of the case felt strangely warm. She set it down on the edge of the table and bent over to study its incongruous inhabitant.

The scorpion was skewed into one of the corners, its tail and stinger curved against a lump of bark. It was one of the big black ones, with large domes on its pincers like shields. It wasn't moving at all and she wondered if it was in some kind of chilled stupor. There was a couple of centimetres of sand in the bottom of the case, with a few insect husks scattered around – dinner. Alice could see a black plastic sheet partially submerged in the sand, with a couple of wires linked to a battery pack in the corner. She figured the sheet must be generating the small amount of heat she could feel, surely necessary to keep a desert dweller like this alive in such freezing conditions.

She returned to the alcove and, with greater difficulty, lifted the large tank containing the snake. Setting that down on the table beside the scorpion, she saw that it was a long, thin snake, brown with albino patches. She wasn't sure, but thought it might be a corn or king snake, one of those non-poisonous types you got in pet stores. Perhaps the S-Js were using it just for symbolism. The tank also contained a heating mat, together with a small bowl of water.

What were we humans doing on this earth?

Alice lifted the larger tank, seeing the snake start to slip about, its face lively against the glass. She set it down right underneath the overhead opening. Then she placed the scorpion's tank on top of it. She looked up and down, gauging the distance.

The ceiling was low, she knew she would be able to reach the opening standing on the tanks and stretching. And she was sure the tanks themselves were sturdy enough to hold her weight.

She tried it. Wobbling slightly. Then straightening. She stretched up, easily touching the old bricks around the edges of the slit. She rummaged in the crevices for any looseness in the mortar. Her fingers were so numb she might just as well have been feeling around with sticks.

The bricks were tight. She stepped down and, realising that her fingers were just too cold, spent five minutes with her hands pressed against the warmest section of the scorpion tank. She wondered how long the batteries would last, how long Jerry had left them down here. She guessed he must have put them down here recently, perhaps this morning. They would certainly be dead otherwise.

She moved the tanks further up the slot and tried the mortar in the next section.

Then the next. This time, the first brick she tugged fell, bringing more with it as well as all the snow that had been bridging the gap. There was a kind of deep crumpling sound followed by a bang as one of the bricks struck the tank. Alice jumped away in a shower of snow and ice.

She checked the tanks to make sure they hadn't broken. The last thing she needed was a venomous companion in her new dungeon. The tanks were strewn with dirt and snow but neither had cracked. She looked up at the newly grown gap.

It was big enough! She could definitely get through that – provided she could get a grip on something strong enough to enable leverage. She could also see that the zigzag crack had grown considerably, releasing a number of bricks too. She wondered just how stable this old structure was.

Alice bent down and wiped the muck and lime mortar off the tanks, briefly imagining the Roman – soldier or slave? – who must have mixed it. Then she realigned the tanks and stepped up on them. Remembering how Jerry had shaped the gap, sloping on either side, she dug her fingers into the snowy soil above the ceiling bricks. She was hoping to grip on to the top edge of the remaining bricks, but there were none exposed to hold. Should she dig away more soil from the top of the roof?

She couldn't imagine it. Her fingers were too cold. And how could she pull herself up by her arms alone? She needed to get her body up higher…

She looked around at the fallen bricks. Six of them. Well, five-and-a-half, just about. She stooped to pick them up and set them on top of the scorpion, three on top of two. That gave her another foot. Not enough.

The plates.

She got the five plates off the table and set them on top of the bricks. Then she stepped back and looked at her stack.

Precarious, at best.

And she probably only had one chance before it all smashed to pieces.

Don't overthink it.

She was just about to step up on to the snake tank when she stopped, aware of someone – *something* – else in the room.

She looked around quickly, into the darkness.

What was it? Why did she feel sure something had been there?

Something watching her…

'Hello?' she said.

Suddenly he was there, standing just a few feet away from her.

The boy in the burgundy hood.

In the dim light, she saw his keen, small eyes staring up at her. Looking sharply at her. Into her.

Alice thought, bringing herself back into the moment. When she finally spoke, it was with the carefulness of a horse whisperer, someone trying to calm a wild animal.

'I can see now, why you were trying to bring me here. Petey.'

His head jerked up when she spoke his name, making her jump.

'You wanted to show me this place. The terrible place where… where they killed her. Where they killed your mum.'

The light was poor, but she could feel the awful penetration of his gaze. A child's gaze, which had seen too much.

'You did well, Petey,' she said. 'You did very well. I'm sorry it took me so long. But now – now you've done what you need to do. I'm going to get out, and I'm going to make sure they pay for all that they did to her. All they did to your mum.'

Was he crying? She could see the movement on his cheeks, his lips tightening. Was he trying to keep a brave face?

'But listen, Petey. There's one more thing. Your mum – she is still here. Like you. You might not see her, but I do. She's here – because she wants you to know how sorry she was. How sad she is that she didn't look after you all the time. Particularly on that horrible day at the lake, when the accident happened.'

He shuffled a little, dipped his head beneath his red hood.

'Petey. She needs to be with you again, to feel you. I don't know how to do it. But maybe… there's a connection between us – between me and your mum now. She's been visiting me. We have – shared our thoughts and feelings.'

As she spoke, Alice could remember the moments vividly, being on the inside of – what? On the inside of a ghost's mind. A woman's mind. Somehow, now, they were attached, she and Mary. She remembered suddenly, vividly, the mysterious pressure she had felt after her mum had died, like something, an entity, was trying to force itself out from behind her eyes. The experience that had made her babble incoherently, feeling as if she was about to give birth – the experience that ended in her writing down the single word, *hope*.

She realized that Mary's ghost was somehow bound to herself, to her light, her life source. It was what was keeping her here, Alice was the one who would… bear witness to her suffering. Help her. She could feel it – her – almost nudging somewhere at her mind, her being.

'Maybe if you just think of her now,' she said to the boy. 'Think of her – and I'll think of her too.'

*What was she doing?* She should be getting out, climbing up through the gap – Jerry could be back at any moment!

But… she needed to do this first.

She had made a connection with Mary. Twice now she had – what? – *merged* with her. Felt her feelings. Felt her pain. If she could… very quietly, very softly… feel it again. *She imagined being in the small room, the garderobe off the bedroom, hearing the crack, the splash… going to the window… seeing the sunlit lawn, vivid green, the lake shimmering… running across the lawn… the shape, the body, floating in the lake…*

The terror and the pain. She felt her face breaking up, wracking with pain, tears flooding down her cheeks.

The pain, too much…

She felt herself being more, being overlapped, her own memories of her ghosts, of this ghost, wrapping up, twisting around each other. She felt the curious, fiery consciousness of another, like a whip inside.

When she opened her eyes, Mary was there.


87


But the ghost was not looking at her. She was looking down at her son, beside her, who was staring back up at her.

Alice watched as the two gazed intently at each other. Neither cried – could ghosts cry? – but both looked calm, intent, in a kind of ethereal rapture as they absorbed each other.

Mary reached up and touched the side of Petey's face. And then they were gone.

## 88

For a moment, Alice stood there in awe. What was that expression she'd heard those TV psychics use… crossing over? Had the ghosts crossed over?

She guessed she would never know for sure.

And then she remembered her situation, the desperation.

She had to get out of this place – now!

She stepped up on the snake tank with her right foot, raised her other foot on top of the ceramic plates, then launched herself upwards at the slit.

She came up high, out into daylight, her arms struck at the soil, one hand caught a rock and she pulled, pulled up as hard as she could, her elbow on the soil, she dug down, thrust herself up again, snow showering around her, she gasped, launched her arm higher up the slope, found nothing to grip but somehow, maybe because of the angle, there was a little more leverage and she pushed, an elbow knocking hard against the rock she'd just held, her stomach now above the bricks, on the snow, she even thrust down with her stomach muscles, her legs kicking in thin air below, then like a snake she swerved, slipped, screeched, terrified as she slipped backwards, then somehow, somehow she rose a knee up, pushed it against the solid edge of the roof and used her arm to shove herself on to her back on the other side of the vent – and then her left knee was up alongside her right and they were jammed against the hard bricks of the roof, stopping her slipping back into the hole and –

She was out!

She looked up at the high branches of the trees above her, black ribbons against a grey sky. A crow flapped by. She breathed deeply, mist forming in front of her eyes.

She was out…

She glanced back down and thought about the ghosts. Were they mended?

Her knees and elbows hurt and she realised she had ripped one of her nails getting out. She turned away so as not to look at the blood. Then, carefully, she shifted her weight on to one side to secure her position and enable her to remove her right knee. She lifted her leg and set her foot on the brick edge, then pushed herself up.

A load more bricks gave way, crashing with a fall of soil into the room below. For a second, she thought the whole roof would give way, and then she was climbing up and out of the vent. Moments later, she was standing staring down at the stumpery.

She was out!

## 89

The giddy moment of exhilaration passed.

What kind of hell had she found herself in? She needed to escape Bramley, all its horror and weirdness, as quickly as possible. She didn't have her phone and she was sure Jerry would have taken her car keys – wouldn't he? Should she go down to the drive and check?

The trouble was, doing so would put her in plain sight of the house and most of the gardens. She might be OK if by some miracle he'd left the keys in the car and she could get away fast. But if he hadn't she was taking a massive risk.

She looked at the yew tree roots all around her, delicately traced with snow.

Of course! She could head away from the house and gardens, through the woods to the upper field. Then, it was at most half a mile to Tom Gauge's farm. Tom would be able to help her!

Footprints in the snow.

She must make sure to cover her tracks.

If Jerry looked down the vent, the disturbance of snow and broken section of roof would tell him she'd got out. She had no way of covering it up. However, there was little reason for him to do so. He would be far more likely to head straight for the door. She just had to make sure that, when he realised she was gone, he didn't know which way.

She had to get into the holly. It was only a few strides away. She picked up a stick and then, on tiptoes, took one, two, three steps towards the bushes and then stopped. Turning back, she used the stick to cover her prints with fresh snow. It wasn't brilliant, but he was unlikely to spot it unless he was looking carefully. She took another three steps, covering her footprints each time, and then thrust herself into the holly.

She made her way through the clump of holly with great difficulty, mostly on her hands and knees, pulling her coat up over her head to avoid getting horribly scratched.

Eventually, she came out on the far side, up the bank, well above the stumpery and temple. From here, she would just have to hope he didn't find her footprints. And that, if he did, she would have such a good start on him that it wouldn't matter. The police would be on their way.

As fast as she could, Alice ran off through the snowy woods towards Tom Gauge's farm.

## 90

When she broke out of the trees at the top of the valley Alice saw the bull.

It was standing in the middle of the upper field. The afternoon light was beginning to fade, but the bull was still distinct, rust-red against the luminous snow. Its breath fogged in front of it, each cloud vanishing close to the ground.

The bull paid her no attention as she hurried along the fence, then made her way up the frosty hedge to the road. There – she could see the stand of pines now, at the bottom of a shallow incline, on the other side of the road. Her finger where she'd ripped the nail was really hurting. She checked nervously left and right for traffic.

Then ran down the lane, tears pricking her eyes.

## 91

Alice gasped with relief as she saw the crooked sign for Aldermans nailed into the wall.

She ran through the gateway, down the drive, through the shadow of the pines, and out into the forecourt of the farm. She ran past the outhouses, past the snow-covered cars, the Land Rover, beige Ford and flat-tyred sports car, up to the main farmhouse.

As she approached the front door of the grey building she panicked for a moment, wondering what she would do if Tom wasn't there. Perhaps he was out on the land, clearing ditches or planting hedges. But then she noticed a soft light in one of the downstairs windows. He must be home!

She banged hard on the door before noticing the bell, which she pushed too.

She waited, scarcely able to breathe, her hands quaking with cold and fear.

'Thank God,' she said, as she heard a thump inside, someone coming.

There was the sound of a latch being turned, and then the door swung inward. Tom was there, in a checked shirt and jeans.

'Oh thank God,' she repeated, stumbling forward into him.

'Alice, what is it?' he said, catching her, holding on to stop her from falling.

'Tom – Tom,' she said, choking on her tears.

'What is it? My God, Alice, what happened?'

'George – Jerry – there's an old temple – he hit me…'

'Jesus, Alice, you're scaring me,' he said. 'Come in, come in.'

'They're a cult,' she said, as he led her down the hall towards an open doorway at the end. She could see part of a table, an Aga, the kitchen.

'Who's a cult?' he said.

'The Smythe-Johnstones – Jerry, the gardener, he's their son. He attacked me and locked me in an underground temple. They're planning to kill me, they – they killed someone else, Mary, they think – oh my God

– they believe *Mithras* will intervene to save Bramley for them…'

'Mithras?'

'A Roman god. The family had an ancestor who found the Temple, I think he probably started it – started their cult. You do believe me…' she said, feeling the unreality of what she was saying, now she was back in such a normal setting.

'Of course I do,' he said, as they came into the warm kitchen.

'We both do.'

Alice froze at the sound of another voice. A familiar voice.

She turned and looked down the room to the speaker who was sitting in an armchair, a small kitten on her lap.

Fran.


92


'What are you doing here?' said Alice.

'You mean, what am I doing in my own house?' said Fran.

Alice glanced at Tom. The farmer put his arm on her shoulder and smiled.

'What the…?' she whispered.

'Fran is my wife,' he said.

'What?'

'Married happily – mostly – for fifteen years,' said Fran, winking at Tom.

Alice looked around. The kitchen was shrinking down, the details, newspaper, neon light, all swimming away, fading, becoming peripheral. Her entire attention focused on a stone fruit bowl on the table. Roughly fashioned. Heavy.

She lunged away from Tom's grasp, reaching for the bowl, snatching it with both hands. She swung it at the large man but he caught her arms by the wrists, shook hard, and the bowl thumped on the ground between them.

Keeping hold of one of her wrists Tom spun her round and twisted it up into the small of her back. Alice tried to pull away but gasped in agony, unable to move.

'What are you doing?' she said.

Fran stood up, setting the kitten down on the floor.

'Taking you back,' she said.

'Shall I call your Dad?' said Tom, looking at Fran.

'Yes,' said Fran. 'Let's get it done.'

'My God,' whispered Alice, staring at Fran. 'You're their daughter…'

'You getting the bull?' said Tom to Fran.

# *Tauroctony Plus*

## 93

'Delicious pie, Heliodromus.'

'Thank you, Pater.'

In the candle-lit underground chamber, cutlery clinked against ceramic. There was a slurping sound as one of the diners drank some wine. Followed by a cough, and then more chewing.

Beneath the altar, Alice lay on her side, her hands tied and masking tape stuck over her mouth and round the back of her head, snagging her hair. Like a creature stunned, she gazed up at the statue of Mithras above her, his blank egg eyes, his dagger thrust out into air. And then she gazed at the table where the Smythe-Johnstones – and their guests – ate.

They scarcely seemed themselves now.

Bernard, at the near end of the table, in profile to her, was wearing a large red-stoned ring and a grey robe. A shepherd's crook was propped against the table beside him. Opposite him was Jerry, who they were calling Heliodromus. His hair was free, frizzy, and he appeared to be wearing eyeliner. He had a stick, or perhaps it was a horse whip, tucked into his belt. He was also wearing a taupe robe, like his father. Further down the table, Samantha was wearing some kind of headband or diadem. Even in the candlelight Alice could see she had managed to get gravy on her cheek. Opposite her was the burly farmer, Tom Gauge, wearing a World War 2 soldier's tin helmet. Samantha was referring to him throughout the dinner as *Mee-lays,* which Alice vaguely thought might be the Latin for soldier. *Miles.* He was calling her Nymph, and feeding tidbits from the table to the black Labrador who sat patiently beside him. Beyond Tom there was one more man, very tall, also wearing a helmet, although his appeared to be a Roman soldier's. Alice knew she had seen him somewhere before, but couldn't...

*David Bridge.* That's who it was. The Committee member who'd come to catalogue the paintings. Or rather, so-called Committee member. Alice wondered who he really was, surely just another uncle, or brother, or cousin of this crazy, crazy family. With her cheek against the stone floor she sneered, thinking how easy it was to research things like the National Committee on the Trust for England website. Fleshing it out with details that you could be sure no one would ever bother to check.

They were all mad. Utterly insane.

Overhead, for a while now, Alice had heard a dull, erratic thumping, occasional snorts. Short booming cries from a woman, who she knew was Fran. She was moving the bull, with a pole from Tom's car in its nose ring.

Alice wasn't scared now. She panicked and fought at first, but after Tom had bound and gagged her, driven her round to Bramley in the back of his Land Rover, she had begun to feel a strange lethargy. There was nothing she could do. She was powerless, unable to move, unable to escape, outnumbered. For a while she had entertained a desperate hope that the Regional Manager – the real

Regional Manager – might be sufficiently disturbed to contact the police and ask them to investigate. But then she realised that, in the unlikely event he did, there was virtually no chance of them rescuing her. Even if Jerry had left her car outside the house with its smashed windscreen, what was the likelihood of them finding her here, hidden in this underground vault?

Zero. There was no chance.

She was done for. She thought about wildlife documentaries she'd watched, when the gazelle was taken down by the lion, or the zebra brought low by a pack of African dogs. There was always a moment when the fear in the prey's eyes went, replaced by a calmer, more distant look of resignation.

That was her, now.

There was nothing she could do. She knew they were mad, they had created their own perversion of faith, a cult based on their own needs. They had not acknowledged the traditions of this mysterious deity, Mithras, the mutual friendship and protection that its all-male initiates coalesced around. The bull had never been killed like this, soaking the initiate, that was a falsehood perpetuated by a rival religion. Even she had read about that. And…

No human sacrifice. There was no human sacrifice to Mithras. Ever.

Overhead, there was a sudden mighty groan followed by a great thump. A pile of soil, stone and rubble crashed down on top of her, so for a moment she thought again that the roof was coming down and this was it, the end even more sudden than she'd expected.

But then it stopped and she realised it was going to hold.

Fran had finally manoeuvred the gigantic bull into the vent.

## 94

Above, the bull grunted and lowed, the noise muffled only slightly by the compacted earth and brick between them.

The door at the end of the temple opened and Fran came in. She too had changed and was now dressed like the others in a greyish robe. On top of her head, slanting to one side, was the Phrygian cap.

'Bull's ready, Pater' she said. She looked exhausted.

'Time to prepare her, then,' said Jerry, looking at Alice.

The diners all stopped eating and clambered off the stone benches. They straightened and turned to face the front. Henry lifted his backside and stood beside Tom, drool hanging from the side of his mouth.

Alice heard a scraping sound, saw Fran near the table, caught a glimpse of a long knife in her hand as she returned to the door. Up above them, the bull bellowed into the snowy woods.

'Who is the Father?' said Bernard, taking up his crook and stepping towards her.

'He who begets everything,' said Jerry, stepping forward too.

Alice tried to gasp, to scream, but the only sound she could make was a nasal drone, like blowing through a paper comb.

'Why are you Pater?' said Jerry.

'It is the will of the Father,' said Tom, Samantha and David, all coming up behind the two men.

As they drew near, Jerry broke formation and crossed to the two tanks. They had been repositioned in the alcove, which was now lit by dozens of tealights set on ledges and around the statue.

Henry trotted out of line, coming up and licking Alice's cheeks. She squeezed her eyes shut and wriggled backwards. His breath smelt of tin. Rank tin.

Suddenly there was a loud but muffled cry from Fran above. The bull's lowing increased in intensity.

'Get back everyone,' said Jerry, stepping deeper into the alcove.

'Ready?' shouted Fran.

'Hold on,' yelled Tom.

'Get back, Henry,' shouted Samantha, tugging the Labrador back from Alice by its collar.

'Move her down a bit,' said Tom. He and Bernard pulled Alice back from the altar, below the edge of the overhead slit, which was still blocked by the bull.

'OK!' shouted Bernard.

There was another cry from Fran and suddenly the bull's frantic lowing ceased. Moments later, a few splashes of black liquid began to drop from above. Terror returned for Alice as she saw the liquid strike the brick floor, then one, two, three spots landed on her coat. She tried to kick herself backwards, towards the altar, but Tom quickly bent and shoved her back into place. The liquid slowed to a few long, intermittent drops for a moment.

And then turned into a fast, steady flow, pouring straight down on to Alice's upper torso, covering her face and hair in the thick, treacly substance.

The dark blood of the slaughtered bull.

<br>

## 95

On the ground, Alice twisted, kicked and reeled as the blood flowed down.

She tried to keep her eyes shut tight, but her instinct was to open them, meaning they ended up being splashed with the viscose fluid. The blood was full of grit and soil, at one stage she even felt something hard strike her back, a stone or brick perhaps. Tom, the false friend, kept stepping in to push her back into position and prevent her from cracking her head on the altar. She fumed and raged against her sticky gag. Once again she found herself completely lost to herself, as if she had gone away to a small room inside her head. She was still there, but the madness and hysteria washed and raged all around her. But not through her. It was not part of her.

The ordeal seemed to last for hours, but it was probably no more than a minute or so before the stream slowed to long drips, then the occasional splat. Dimly, she heard crunching sounds, as the bull continued to spasm, his great hooves striking the roof and sending down showers of stone and soil.

Alice opened her eyes, blinked away the blood. She was dimly aware that Fran was now back in the room with them.

'The Saviour has arrived,' said Bernard, holding his hand out above her. She could see his ring, a ruby set in brass or gold. In the hand gleamed a short, sharp knife.

'He knows what we need,' he added.

There were noises behind, she twisted her head off the ground to catch a glimpse of Jerry stooping down behind her. There was a tugging as he freed her hands. Next, Tom knelt beside her in his blood-soaked robe, tin helmet aslant on his head. He grabbed her by the side and lifted her up. Someone took her hand and, twisting her head around, she saw Jerry thrust it down into the smaller of the tanks.

She tried to scream. There was a sensation on the back of her hand, like someone had tapped it. It was immediately followed by a sharp, agonising pain. Alice kicked Samantha, and the old woman cried out.

There was more scraping behind her, followed by a clicking sound. She knew what it was. Tears were streaking her cheeks, rivulets made through the blood. She could see Samantha holding an open tin of... dog food.

What...?

She was trying to shout at them, to tell them that they were all mad, that they would be caught, that the Trust for England knew something was up now, that she would be missed by Matthew, surely –

But nothing came out.

She became aware of a dance, a hula hoop, no, a line in the air...

The snake, held from above, was angry, striking wildly about.

Her coat was pulled away and she was shoved towards the twisting, livid creature.

The snake danced, bounced, shook and then struck her on the top of her shoulder.

Then Alice screamed as Bernard stepped towards her, his knife raised high above his head.

## 96

And then time seemed to slow down, and several things happened at once.

Watching the old man's face, Alice became aware of a change in his expression, from careless determination to surprise, and then to terror. Turning her head slightly, she realised what he had seen, the wounded woman, Mary Stevens, surging forward, shrieking – *silently* shrieking – at him, her face distorted with the long-stored hatred of the dead and grieving. Bernard staggered backwards, stumbling towards the table as Alice heard a deep, crumpled groaning above and at the same time felt the faintest presence beside her, a safe presence, and turning found herself staring straight into the eyes of the ghost boy, Petey, the boy in the burgundy hood, who beckoned her swiftly so she dived towards him, past the altar into the recessed alcove behind Mithras, and the noise from above grew louder and those around her, Samantha, Tom, David, Fran, Jerry and barking Henry, and behind them Bernard still screeching at the revenant, all looked up as unseen above the spasming bull gave a final, powerful, beastly kick, and with a great crunch…

The roof of the temple fell in.

## 97

She opened her eyes and looked up into daylight.

She saw black trees, white snow, grey sky.

She was lying diagonally across rocks – no, bricks. And mud.

Her legs and her hand and her right shoulder hurt terribly. She looked down at her body. For a moment she panicked at all the blood – surely she was going to die? – and then remembered the bull. Most of it was not hers. But her aching right leg was under rubble. In fear she pulled it up. There was more pain, a sharp jab in the knee, but it came free. She twisted around on to her side and then realised fully what had happened.

Beside her, she could see the top of Mithras' head and his broken forearm, protruding from a huge pile of brick, earth and snow. In the midst of the rubble she could see the russet flank of the bull, but its head was somehow concealed. There was no sign of the family and Alice knew that they were all down there, crushed beneath the wreckage of the ancient temple.

She ripped off the tape from her mouth, ignoring the flash of pain on her skin and from the hairs coming out.

Then she leaned her head against the shattered arm of Mithras and wept.

## 98

Sometime later, she felt a presence again, a cold fingering of wind at the back of her neck although the winter scene was still.

She looked up and they were there.

Mary – and her son.

Together, the ghosts moved across the wreck of the temple towards her in the soft afternoon light. They stopped, staring down at her. Looking at them both now, calm, side by side, Alice expected to see the family resemblance. But, as is often the case, there was none. Mary had a yellowish, dusky hint to her skin, large eyes, full lips. Petey was pink-skinned with strawberry-blond hair and a thin, drawn mouth. The bone structure of his face was chiselled, his eyes small and darting, as if anticipating danger from any quarter.

But there was one similarity, in their expressions, their demeanour, the way they stood – the deep hunger, or *lack*, in their eyes.

They had both lived lives immeasurably more difficult than most.

'Thank you,' Alice whispered to Petey.

The two ghosts stared down at her. Despite there being no merging of thoughts, Alice could still feel something, an aura, coming off them. She knew she had somehow helped them past their painful ties – to guilt, to anger – and they…

They, in the end, had saved her too.

## 99

After a while, she realised that the ghosts were gone.

Alice looked sideways at the pupil-less eyes of Mithras, gazing off into the woods for the first time ever.

Then, slowly, she clambered to her feet, ignoring the shooting pains all over her body.

She began to make her way back towards the house.

# The Role

## 100

*To:* Jane Deaton

*Friday 13 Apr: 16.31*
Hi Mum, are you there?

*Saturday 14 Apr: 14.12*
I should have listened to you

*Sunday 15 Apr: 00.45*
I am so scared

*Sunday 15 Apr: 13.55*
Mum, are you out there? Do you see the others? Dad? Mary, her son? Are they there with you?

*Thursday 19 Apr: 09.34*
Mum please speak to me. I can't stand all this publicity, it's a freak show. I could tell them everything but they'd lock me up. I have to keep them, Mary and Petey, secret, keep to a simple story. The crazy family cult. Mum?

*Thursday 19 Apr: 10.33*
I don't know what to do

*Friday 20 Apr: 23.11*
Mum I miss you. Thank you for – what do you call it? – staying back for me. I know your job is done, and done well. I love you, mum.

*Monday 23 July: 20.50*
I've seen him again, mum. Just in case you can still hear me. The man, the reader – the one I told you about in those last few days we had together. You remember? He told me what to do. We help each other now. They help me, I help them.


## 101

Finally, on a bright summer's day, when all was over, she made the four-hour drive north to Loveton. She parked her car by the village pond and, after watching a pair of dragonflies jerk about above the yellow irises, walked over to the small Norman church. She passed under the kissing gate with its trumpeting, still faintly painted angels, and made her way through the churchyard with its sun-filled patches of wildflowers.

Round the far side, in the afternoon shade of the spire, she found the small stone set in the turf, four down from the cherry tree.

It was the one thing she had been determined to stay involved with. Following a forensic search of the grounds, the bones of both mother and son had been discovered in a clearing in the Bramley woodland – a place that Alice had once thought would make a lovely spot for a small play area.

The Police Superintendent, a young Asian man, had clearly been surprised by Alice's request upon hearing of the discovery. Since the defendants were all deceased there was no trial, but after the coroner's report the Superintendent had referred her to the local council. There she found out that, following an unsuccessful search for relatives, they were preparing to have the bones cremated and scattered in a garden of remembrance.

When Alice offered to pay for the headstone and a lot in the church grounds, the authorities agreed to let her take the ashes. So she had attended the sad, quiet ceremony, and been successful in her determination not to cry. Then she had taken the urn away with her and delivered them to St Mary's – so beautiful the link of the name – in Loveton.

Now, she stood above the small, rectangular stone. Someone, a thin old man with a broad-brimmed sunhat, was tending another grave, a dozen yards away. She didn't expect any tears but put on her sunglasses, just in case.

*Mary and Petey Stevens*
*Mother and son, ages unknown*
*Buried here on 4$^{th}$ May 2019*

*In death you are as one*

In death you are as one.

It was all she had been able to think of. It felt so inadequate for everything they had endured. Surely she could have done better?

And then tears were flooding down her cheeks, so that she was glad she was wearing the glasses. Still at one stage she let out a single loud sob and the elderly man evidently heard her because he got up and walked over to her.

'Are you all right, my dear?' he asked.

His accent was lovely, so kind, so English.

She nodded.

'I will be,' she said.

## *Epilogue*

### *Three Years Later*

'Hurry up, Oliver!'

Oliver was intent on his ice cream tub. He was whipping the plastic spoon around in circles, making himself a sweet creamy soup. DEE-LISH-US.

'Oliver, the tour starts in three minutes and I don't want to miss it.'

'I'm coming.'

His mother grabbed him by the top of his arm and pulled him up from the table.

'Hey!' he protested, still trying to get the slop into his mouth. The smear he left across his freckled cheek was swiftly erased by his mum's palm.

'Come on!'

Begrudgingly he allowed himself to be marshalled from the bright, high-ceilinged café, past an elderly couple sharing a slice of cream cake and gazing vacantly past each other.

'I want to see the knight,' he said, as his mum urged him towards the door. He loved the knight, his helmet was so smooth, he wanted to touch the sword although he'd been told repeatedly he wasn't allowed to touch anything in here.

'Later,' said his mother. Reluctantly, he allowed her to lead him away, out down a cool corridor and through a small door into the dazzling light where a group of people were gathering.

Oliver looked up into the sun and quickly away, his eyes flashing with black orbs. He stared at the huge white house with its masses of ivy and its clock high, high up on the bell tower. That's two o'clock, he thought, unsure of whether he was right or wrong. Two o'clock was his favourite time, because it was the time his dad had taught him.

'Can I play with the girl?' he said.

'Which girl?' said his mother.

'Her,' said Oliver, pointing.

His mother glanced at the crowd of people.

'I don't see a girl,' she said.

'The one with the big dress.'

'No, shush, be quiet. Here's the lady.'

Oliver looked at the girl and then up at the woman who everyone had turned towards. She was wearing a green top with the deer badge on it, like the other people who worked here. She had a white rectangle badge with letters on it too. Oliver didn't read.

'Hello everyone,' she said. 'My name is Alice. I'm going to be taking you on your tour today. We're going to start by going through Farthingbridge House, seeing the fabulous Gold Room with its Bösendorfer piano and then the State Room, for those lovers of the latest incarnation of Mr Darcy. As we go round, I'll tell you the history of the house, and how it came into the hands of the Trust. Finally, we'll head out into the grounds and I'll show you the hallmark features of the Capability Brown landscape, the Grecian Temple and the boat lake. And, as it's nearly Halloween, for those of you with a taste for the macabre, we'll see the place where Lord Ashford committed his terrible crimes.'

'Don't the revisionists think it was Berwick, his servant?' said a man with a green scarf wrapped twice round his neck. Oliver thought he looked like a toad.

'Oh no, they're wrong,' said the lady. 'Lord Ashford was a monster. I can tell you that for sure.'

'Can you really?' said the man. 'I hope you'll be sharing all the gory details.'

The woman looked at him sharply. 'We have to bear in mind the children,' she said.

Oliver saw how, after her fiery look at the man, the woman glanced down at him, and then looked to his side. Turning his head, Oliver realised that the girl in the shiny dress was now standing beside him. He looked at the side of her face and saw how she was older than him, and how she had a nasty cut on her cheek. She had blond hair, curly at the ends, and she looked angry. Very angry. And spiteful.

Oliver decided he didn't want to play with the girl after all.

*Thank you for reading this book. If you enjoyed it, please consider telling your friends or leaving a review. Word of mouth is an author's best friend and much appreciated.*

## *About the Author*

Steve Griffin is a poet and novelist. His travels around India, Africa and America – combined with the discovery of a magical *garden of rooms* buried deep in the Herefordshire countryside – inspired him to write his adventure mystery series, *The Secret of the Tirthas*. The first book in the series, *The City of Light*, was described in *The Guardian* as 'entertaining and exciting'. Steve's poetry has been published in anthologies and magazines including *Poetry Ireland, Rialto* and *Poetry Scotland*. His first poetry collection, *Up in the Air*, came out in 2018.

Steve lives in the Surrey Hills with his wife and two sons.

To hear about new writing, please email stevegriffin40@outlook.com to subscribe to his mailing list. You can also find out more at steve-griffin.com, and connect with him using the handle @stevegriffin.author on Instagram and Facebook.

Printed in Poland
by Amazon Fulfillment
Poland Sp. z o.o., Wrocław

50954439R00136